BOURTON-ON-THE-WATER'S

Mystery Of The
Model Village

BOURTON-ON-THE-WATER'S

Mystery Of The Model Village

Number Three in The Amazing
Alpacas Adventure Series

David Wiemers

Wavyline Publishing

First published in Great Britain
in 2010 by Wavyline Publishing.

Author David Wiemers
Illustrator Robin Edmonds
Cover design Richard Jervis

A CIP catalogue record for this book
is available from the British Library.

ISBN 978-0-9550606-1-8

www. Fluffandhisfriends.com

*Printed and bound in Great Britain by
CPI Cox & Wyman, Reading, England*

The Author

DAVID WIEMERS is an Emmy-award-winning comedy writer and producer. He has worked on many of America's favourite television programmes, such as "Cheers," "Major Dad," "Coach," "Ducktales," and "Harry and the Hendersons."

During his 25-year career in Hollywood he was under contract by all the major studios, including, The Walt Disney Company, Universal Studios, Paramount Studios and Warner Brothers.

During this period he was nominated for 5 Emmy awards and he won the coveted prize in 1988 for "Jim Henson's Muppet Babies".

Having written and produced over 150 television comedy series, David has worked with many of Hollywood's top celebrities.

In 2002, David moved from the USA to Bourton-on-the-Water in Gloucestershire, England. During his time living in Bourton he owned several businesses, including the Bourton-on-the-Water Post Office and the Bourton Coffee Company. During this period he was also the subject of several BBC documentaries, including "Heaven and Earth" and "Live at Chatsworth".

In 2008, David and his family returned to the United States. They currently reside near San Diego, California.

Contents

This book is dedicated to all the
Camels, Llamas,
Guanacos, Vicunas
and Alpacas living on this wonderful planet.

Prologue

To be honest, I didn't know what a prologue was. My Dad told me to put this in. He said that it's stuff the reader needs to know before I tell my story. Okay, so here goes . . .

My best friend Roy talks to his alpacas and they totally understand him. And his alpacas snort and hum and squeal, and he understands them perfectly. It's amazing. When they talk he says it's called Pacachatter. Roy didn't learn Pacachatter in Alpaca School or anything – it happened one day when a bolt of lightning struck them all. I'm serious. It was so bizarre. Okay, here's what went down...

It all started with a bag of fertilizer. The warning on the bag was real clear. It said: "Warning: never, under any circumstances, should this bag of Uncle Mick's Special and Unique Home-grown Fertilizer be exposed to electricity. This includes electrical charges, electrical currents, electric fields, electromagnetism, and electrical thunderstorms, especially thunderstorms that occur in England in the lovely and delightful area known as the Cotswolds."

Roy and his family, the Keatings, live on Hillcote Farm – it's up on Clapton Hill above Bourton-on-the-Water in the lovely and delightful area known as the Cotswolds. They had a bag of Uncle Mick's fertilizer hanging around. But did anyone bother to read the warning?

No!

There's even a warning at the website:

---

www.UncleMicksSpecialandUniqueHomegrownFertilizer.stuff

"The danger is even more extreme when Uncle Mick's Special and Unique Home-grown Fertilizer is exposed to thunderstorms in the Cotswolds during a total eclipse of the sun."

But did anyone at Hillcote Farm go to this website and read this?

No!

Did anyone at Hillcote Farm google to find out if alpaca fleece goes bonkers during an electrical thunderstorm in the lovely and delightful area known as the Cotswolds during a total eclipse of the sun?

Of course not.

So it's a no-brainer that when an electrical thunderstorm came on the same day as a total eclipse of the sun in the lovely and delightful area known as the Cotswolds that something major was about to explode.

It all happened one August afternoon when Mother Nature was in a seriously bad mood. She whipped up a terrible electrical thunderstorm and served it to everyone, whether they wanted it or not.

So, since a storm was coming, Roy went out to the paddocks to bring in their three alpacas. You see, the Keatings raise alpacas because they're nice animals and, oh yeah, their fleece is worth tons of money. Roy said the rain was coming down like darts and he was the dartboard. When he finally found the alpacas, they were running around in circles and behaving like crazies in the storm. He shouted, "Follow me," but the alpacas just kept running in circles, because alpacas don't understand English, right?

Finally, Roy got the alpacas to follow him, and on the way back he found this little sheep that had wandered away from its flock. Roy felt sorry for the little guy because he was stinking wet (and, believe me, when sheep are wet, they stink!) So he told the sheep to join them, but it just said, "Baa," because sheep don't speak English either, right?

"Roy! Roy!! Where are you, son?"

Roy could hear his father, back at the barn, calling him, but the storm was worse than ever and the barn was still a long way away. That's when the lightning started. Talk about snap, crackle, pop! Roy pushed and shoved and begged the animals to get out of the rain and into a barn.

There was another bolt of lightning and Roy looked up to see this weird thing in the sky. He said that it looked like the moon with a halo around it. (Later, we figured out that this was the eclipse of the sun.) So, anyway, Roy shouted to the three alpacas and one sheep, "Hurry!"

As they raced towards the barn, they passed a bag of Uncle Mick's Special and Unique Home-grown Fertilizer and just then a bolt of lightning struck and...

KABOOM!

The next thing Roy remembered was waking up in his bedroom. His Mum and Dad were standing over him with that Oh-we're-so-worried-about-you look on their faces and Dr. Cartle was poking him like he was a science project or something. "How do you feel?"

Roy said, "Fine, I guess, but why are you poking me?"

"Dr. Cartle is making sure you're alright," said Roy's Dad. "Lightning struck the barn and you were very close."

"Gave us quite a scare," said Dr. Cartle, shining a bright light right into his eyes. Blind city!

Once the doctor had finished poking and blinding Roy, he left; Roy's Mum brought him some tea, told him to rest and then left. Roy's Dad is an amateur inventor so he went back to his Shed of Invention to blow something up.

So, anyway, Roy was resting, just lying in bed counting all the cracks on the ceiling, when the alpacas stuck their heads in his bedroom window. Fluff is the leader of the alpacas and he said, "Boy, was that a storm or what?"

Roy said, "Yeah, wicked."

Thumpet said it was the worst storm he had ever seen. "Even worse than in Chile," added Emily. (That's the country where the alpacas come from. I think Chile is near Argentina, but ask your Geography teacher just to be sure.)

Roy yak, yak, yakked with the alpacas, and then he suddenly realized how totally bizarre this was. Were his ears playing tricks on him? Was this a dream? "Wow, since when can you guys talk?" he asked.

Roy told me the alpacas were just as surprised as he was. Fluff said, "Since when can you Pacachatter?"

"Pacachatter? What's that?" asked Roy.

"Yeah, what's that?" asked Thumpet. (The fleece on Thumpet's head isn't protecting much, if you know what I mean.)

"What we're speaking," said Fluff. "Pacachatter. Usually you fleeceless types Fuglechatter."

"Fuglechatter?" asked Roy. "What's that?"

"It's what fugles speak. Fuglechatter. You're a fugle."

"I didn't know that," said Thumpet.

"There's a lot you don't know, Thumpet," said a voice out of nowhere.

"Who said that?" asked Roy, looking around. So did Thumpet.

The other alpacas looked around too, and, with their long

necks, they can really look around! Standing below them was a sheep. "Me. Alfie," he said.

The alpacas were amazed. "Wow, you Pacachatter, too?"

Alfie the sheep said, "And why shouldn't I? I'm an alpaca, too."

The alpacas laughed and hummed and then laughed some more. Roy laughed, too. "You're not an alpaca," he said. "You're a sheep."

Roy told me that remark hurt Alfie's feelings. "I most certainly am not," said the sheep.

Just then, Roy's Mum opened his bedroom door. "Who are you talking to in here?" she asked.

Roy said, "Mum, this is so amazing!" He told her that he could talk to the alpacas and that they could talk to him. "How cool is that?"

Roy's Mum didn't think it was so cool. "Perhaps I let the doctor go too soon," she said, checking his forehead to see if he had a temperature. And then she shut the window to keep the alpacas out. "Now stay in bed and get some rest," she said, and left the room again.

Roy stayed in bed for about a nanosecond. He opened the window again to let his new fleecy friends poke their heads inside. "What did she say?" asked Fluff. "We don't Fuglechatter."

Roy was confused. "Let me get this straight. You understand me, but you don't understand her?"

The alpacas said yes. Well, Thumpet just hummed.

"And I can understand you. But can other animals understand me?" he wondered aloud.

Fluff said, "Let's find out." So Fluff, Emily and Thumpet, the three alpacas, went over to the barn and brought back a donkey and a cockerel. Roy said, "Hey, Mr. Donkey, do you understand what I'm saying?"

The donkey just snorted and brushed its tail back and forth.

He walked back to the barn. "Guess not," said Roy, so he turned to the cockerel and said, "What about you, Mr. Cock-a-doodle-do?"

But the cockerel just walked around in circles and tried to eat bugs. (Kinda like a kid at school named Jason. He's such a gimp.)

So Roy and the alpacas and one sheep who thinks he's an alpaca tried to figure it all out. But it was very complicated. That's when Roy came to me.

My name is Bruce. I'm an American Fugle living in England because my parents dragged me over here a few years ago even though I wanted to stay in Maryland and hang out with my friends. My Dad said, "Don't be ridiculous, you can't stay in Maryland by yourself, you're only seven years old." So now I live with my parents in the lovely and delightful area known as the Cotswolds, but it's pretty cool because that's where I met Roy and now I hang out with him.

So I tried to help Roy figure all this out. But I wasn't much help because I can't Pacachatter with the alpacas or Alfie the sheep who thinks he's an alpaca. (Although my dog Foggy can read me like a book. If I even put on my shoes, he thinks we're going for a walk. He's sharp!)

But Roy is brilliant and he finally figured it all out. (That's why I like hanging out with him, because he thinks of all these amazing things that never seem to land here on Planet Bruce.) He says smart things like, "What do three alpacas, one sheep who thinks he's an alpaca, and I have in common?" Answer: the storm, the lightning, the thunder, the eclipse of the sun, and a bag of fertilizer.

The result? Magic!

Sounded good to me. All I know is that ever since that terrible storm we've been having these amazing adventures.

Two boys, three alpacas and one sheep who thinks he's an alpaca.

The story I'm about to tell you really happened and I'm not making any of it up, I swear. And to think – it all began with a bag of fertilizer!

Chapter One

SOMETHING weird was going on at the Model Village. Something mysterious. My best friend Roy was certain of it. That's because Roy has these amazing alpacas that have a way of sniffing out mysteries.

It's like my dog, Foggy, who has this way of sniffing out a hunt. I take Foggy outside, thinking we're going out for a nice walk. But Foggy sniffs, pulls on his leash and drags me in the direction he wants to go, which is not necessarily the way I want to go. And, sure enough, we soon discover there's a scared rabbit huddled in the corner of some dark shed, or a slice of pizza lying dead by the side of a road.

That's the way it is with Roy's alpacas. They sniff and snort and hum. Their ears perk up. They can smell things that we fugles can't even imagine: fear, danger, mystery, that kind of stuff. That's what happened at the Model Village.

I wish I could. I'm clueless. I'm not as smart as Roy. I thought we were there just to have fun and goof on visitors. ("Hey, my friend Roy is from Turkey. Can you help me? He doesn't speak English. He only gobbles! Ha, ha, ha, ha!!!") Roy, on the other hand, was convinced the alpacas had sniffed out the next great mystery of Bourton-on-the-Water (that's the village where we live.) "The alpacas think they smell a mystery at the Model Village," he said.

"Yeah, right," I said. "What's so mysterious about the Model Village?"

Maybe I should explain. The Model Village is a miniature version of Bourton-on-the-Water. It's 1/9th the size of the real village and, even though it's small, it's a big attraction here in Bourton. You can find it behind The Old New Inn, a hotel and pub here in the real village. Lots of visitors come to Bourton-on-the-Water every year, and most of them end up at the Model Village because they like to pay money to see a smaller version of the village. If you ask me, the real village doesn't take that long to visit and you can see it for free, but I think visitors like The Model Village because it makes them feel so big. You can't help but feel big when you stand next to the Victoria Hall and it only comes up to your knees. In real life, the Victoria Hall is huge! But there's nothing mysterious about it.

Roy disagreed. He said it started when Talonie, the ticket-seller at the Model Village, shouted at the top of her lungs, "We're about to close, so please visit us another day." Talonie is the kind of lady who is oh-so-nice to parents, but mean-and-snotty to kids. She's really big, but her breeches are way too small, so Roy and I call her Miss Too-Tight-Snotty-Breeches.

So, anyway, the rule is that the Model Village closes at exactly five o'clock. You can always tell when it's five o'clock in Bourton-on-the-Water because the bells at St. Lawrence's church bong five times. You can hear it all the way across the village. So Roy and I heard the bells and we started to leave, but just outside the exit turnstile were Roy's alpacas. They had come along with us but had to wait outside because the Model Village, like most places in Bourton, has animal-discrimination rules. No animals inside. Harsh!

Once we got back to the alpacas, Fluff snorted and hummed and was upset about something. Since Roy understands Paca-chatter, he said, "Wow! Really?" He turned to me and said,

"C'mon, we've gotta go back inside and take some more pictures."

Fine by me. I didn't know why but I figured it was better to go back inside than go home and do homework. So we went back inside and Roy took more pictures. Click, click, click. His grandmother, Nan Olga, had just given him a cool new digital camera for his birthday.

So, by now, all the visitors were gone except for Roy and me, and that's when Miss Too-Tight-Snotty-Breeches got all snotty and nearly split her breeches when she said, "Time to go!"

But Roy and I weren't going anywhere. We were too busy taking pictures. Roy said, "Wow, look at that! That wasn't there before. Neither was that. Fluff is right. Something weird is going on here." That's when Miss Too-Tight-Snotty-Breeches stomped over and pointed to the exit. "Out! Now!"

Okay, okay, we can take a hint.

So Roy and I ditched the Model Village and joined the alpacas outside. Fluff snorted and hummed and was full of questions. Ditto Emily. Thumpet was bouncing up and down. Roy spoke to them in Pacachatter and I just stood there feeling stupid. But, hey, I'm used to it. And that's when Roy turned to me and said, "I think the alpacas may be right. Something weird is going on here. Let's go check out the pictures and see what we can find out."

Cool! So we all headed up to Hillcote Farm. Once we were there, Roy and I went to his bedroom, where he downloaded all the pictures from his camera onto his computer. I opened the window for the animals to stick their heads in and see what was going on. Roy turned his monitor so that we could all see.

"Look at this," he said. The picture was of a cottage in the Model Village where a window was open. "Now look at this picture," he said, clicking on another picture of the same cottage taken a few minutes later. The window was closed, the curtains were drawn and a light was on. The alpacas looked at the pictures, too; they blinked and their ears perked up.

"Weird. How do you explain that?" I asked.

"If I knew, it wouldn't be a mystery." He clicked on some other pictures. One was a flat above a shop on the High Street. The next picture, taken like a minute later, showed a light on in the same flat.

The weirdest of all was a picture of the miniature Post Office. In one picture, there was an ugly little bicycle in the alley next to the little Post Office. Yet, in another picture, the bicycle was gone. This was weird, because my parents own the Post Office. Not the one in the Model Village. The one in real life. The big one. We live in a flat above the Post Office. My bedroom is right above the High Street, so from my window I can spy on everyone as they walk by. It's great. But I promise you I would never leave my superior bicycle in the alley because it's so cool someone would steal it in a flash. "So whose ugly little bicycle was that, and where did it go?"

"Good question," said Roy. "And who would turn on lights in the Model Village? I mean, what's the point? No one lives there, right?"

Fluff snorted and hummed. His ears perked up. Roy explained to me, "Fluff thinks little fugles live in the Model Village. He saw shadows. Something or someone dashing inside."

Alfie the sheep bleated, too.

"Alfie agrees because he says a little man ran underneath him on his way inside."

Alfie bleated again.

"He said the top of the man's head tickled his tummy."

I laughed, but Roy didn't. He took this information seriously. He rubbed his chin. "I think we need to investigate this." He sounded very official.

Fluff hummed something.

"What'd he say?" I asked.

"He said the alpacas agree. They want to help, too. What about you? Are you in?"

I have to admit, I had my doubts. This entire mystery was again hanging on the word of a couple of alpacas and one sheep who thinks he's an alpaca. Still, tomorrow was Saturday, and I had nothing better to do. "Sure, I'm in," I said.

"Then meet us back here tomorrow morning at nine o'clock sharp."

"Cool."

I walked back home to the Post Office and had a good laugh. Little people living in the Model Village. Yeah, right. What were their names? Barbie and Ken?

Gimme a break.

Chapter Two

THE next morning I found Roy in the barn feeding the alpacas and the other animals. "What are you doing here already?" he said.

"What do you mean? You told me to be here at nine o'clock." I looked at my watch. Exactly!

"It's only eight o'clock. You forgot to put your watch back, didn't you? Yesterday was the end of summertime."

There was that stupid feeling again. I fixed my watch.

Roy just laughed. "That's okay. Gives us more time to investigate."

Once he'd finished, we were ready to begin our big investigation. "So where do we begin?" I asked, positive that someone as smart as Roy would know.

But Roy scratched his head and said, "I dunno. How would you solve this?"

"Easy," I said. "I'd ask my Dad. He knows everything."

Sounded good to Roy. But since my Dad was all the way down in the village at the Post Office, we decided to start with Roy's Dad, who was right there, in his Shed of Invention. I think I told you already - Roy's Dad, Mr. Keating, is an amateur inventor. He even invented a word for himself: gizmo-monger. He invents gizmos to make life on this planet better. The problem is that most of his gizmos don't work. Like his Rock–A–Bye–Granny – an electric rocking chair that was more rocket than rocking. Hurled poor Granny across the room.

Mr. Keating has lots of big ideas. His latest is called a Super Sheep Sleep 'n' Fleecer, a gizmo that puts sheep to sleep while they're getting their fleece sheared. That's the plan, anyway. Roy's Dad still has a few flaws to work out.

"Dad, have you noticed anything weird going on at the Model Village?"

"Just a minute, son," said Mr. Keating. He threw a switch and – ZAP – a bolt of electricity shot into the headgear. But there was a hitch – Mr. Keating, and not a sheep, was wearing the headgear. In less than an instant, he was asleep. I mean sound asleep. Even faster than my Dad falls asleep after a big meal.

"Dad? Dad?? Can you hear me?"

By now Roy's Dad was snoring. "zzzzZZZZ..." Standing on his feet, but snoring.

Roy turned to the alpacas and me. "Next!" He headed for the door.

"Wait," I said. "What about your Dad? Will he be alright?"

Roy set an alarm clock that his Dad keeps in the Shed of Invention for just this kind of emergency.

Next, the alpacas and Roy and I headed down the hill into Bourton. The Post Office is always busy on Saturday mornings and, if I was going to talk to my Dad, I was going to have to wait in line with all the customers who wanted to see him, too. And there was a line all the way out the door.

Outside the Post Office, there was a lady asking people to sign her petition. "Stop the Victorian Late-night Shopping Event," she said. "Put an end to this foolishness."

I couldn't believe it. Stop the shopping event? The Victorian Late-night Shopping Event is by far the best night of the year. It's always the first Friday of every December and it's the only night when all of the shops and tearooms stay open so that everyone can start their Christmas shopping. The shopkeepers all wear old-fashioned Victorian costumes. And there's this huge Christmas tree that is placed in the middle of the river – I'm not kidding, right in the middle of the river – and when it's all lit up it looks like a giant rocket ship ready to blast off to the North Pole. Father Christmas comes to the village and gives sleigh rides to kids (and even to some of the old guys who are too lazy to walk from one pub to the next). There are Christmas carol singers, and reindeer, and bands playing, and even people selling that dangerous stuff called mistletoe. (Careful: smooches ahead!) I get buzzed just thinking about how much fun it is. (The shopping event, not the mistletoe!) So I couldn't believe anyone would want to stop it from happening.

The lady with the petition was Mrs. Nethercote, an old grouch who lives in the village. She uses a stick to walk with, but sometimes I've seen her use it to threaten people, so I think it's a stick of many uses. She was using it to threaten people to sign her petition. Most of the people ignored her. That's what Roy and I did.

Eventually, the line grew shorter and Roy and I were inside, but the alpacas had to stay outside because even my Dad has harsh animal-discrimination rules. I guess it's because alpacas don't have much money to spend inside. We made our way up to the counter, but the next available person was Amelia, who works with my Dad.

"Can I help you?" she asked.

"Nah, I'll wait for my Dad," I said. "I need to ask him some questions about the Model Village. We think something weird is going on there."

"Nothing weird is going on there, I can assure you," said Amelia. She then leaned forward, and whispered, "Why do you ask?"

Amelia gets weird like this sometimes. She's afraid of her own shadow. But just then my Dad became free, so I asked him the same question.

"Bruce, can't this wait until this evening?"

I guess the look on my face said it all. My Dad just glared at me, then looked to the people still standing in line. "Next!"

So Roy and I decided that the next stop on our investigation should be the Bourton-on-the-Water Tourist Information Office. There's always lots of good information there, but the real reason we went is that Roy's Mum works there. The alpacas went with us, but again they had to stay outside because of − you guessed it - animal-discrimination rules. Roy and I went inside, where old Mrs. Pruitt was talking to Roy's Mum. He said, "Mum, can I ask you some questions?"

"In a minute, dear," said Roy's Mum. "Can't you see I'm talking to Mrs. Pruitt?"

Mrs. Pruitt is an old lady who lives in the village and never goes anywhere without her little shopping trolley. She pushes it everywhere. And into everything. My Dad complains every time she comes into the Post Office. He calls Mrs. Pruitt a one-woman demolition crew.

Roy's Mum was trying to twist Mrs. Pruitt's arm. Not really twist it, but you know what I mean. She said, "Mrs. Pruitt, I would like to ask a special favour of you. Will you be our judge for 'Best Window Display'?"

Mrs. Pruitt smiled and said, "Me? Really? What would I have to do?"

"You'll go from shop to shop and decide which window decoration is the most festive during our Victorian Late-night Shopping Event."

Just the mention of the Victorian Late-night Shopping Event turned Mrs. Pruitt's smile upside down. "Oh. Perhaps you should ask someone else." She pushed her little shopping trolley towards the door.

Roy's Mum blocked the door. "But you'd be such a good judge. Your windows at home are always so festive at Christmas. Besides, others have already turned me down. Won't you help?"

Old Mrs. Pruitt shook her head. "No, not this year. Mrs. Nethercote doesn't think the Victorian Late-night Shopping Event is such a good idea. And I wouldn't want to get on her bad side."

Even though Roy's Mum was smiling, to me she looked like a kettle ready to whistle. "Oh, Mrs. Nethercote is just a big woman with small ideas."

Still, old Mrs. Pruitt said no and left the Tourist Information Office, but not before knocking over a stand of pamphlets with her little shopping trolley. I picked up everything off the floor while Roy dumped a load of questions on his mother. "Mum, do you think anything weird is going on over at the Model Village? Anything mysterious?"

"No," she said. "Why do you ask?"

Roy told her about Fluff seeing shadows and a little man who tickled Alfie when he ran under his tummy and lights going on and off in the tiny cottages at the Model Village. The more he said, the more worried his mother looked. "Oh dear," she sighed. "More tales from the alpacas. I hoped you would have outgrown this by now. Oh dear, oh dear, oh dear..."

Roy is so smart that he knew to change the subject. "Hey, Mum, maybe Mrs. Foote will judge the windows for you. Ask her!" He picked up the phone, handed it to her, and then turned to me and said, "We're outta here!"

Roy and I joined the alpacas outside the Tourist Information Office, which should be renamed Information for Tourists but Not for Kids Office. Roy and the alpacas did their Pacachatter thing.

"What'd they say?" I asked.

"Fluff says that if we want answers to our mystery, we should go back to the Model Village and get them ourselves."

"Really? He said all that with a hum?"

Then Alfie bleated.

"And Alfie thinks we should make it a race."

"Cool." I'd never known a sheep that bleated such good ideas.

Roy quickly put together a route: we were to cross two bridges, run through an alleyway, then go along the river and across the street over to the Old New Inn. "Be careful crossing the street," he said to the animals. "Always check for traffic." By blinking their eyes they promised to be careful. Then we lined up and Roy said in Pacachatter, "Ready, steady, go!"

We were off. We ran like crazy, across the bridge and over the green. The alpacas ran amazingly fast and Alfie ran faster than any sheep I've ever seen, so maybe there's something to be said about thinking like an alpaca. Roy and I ran way behind.

The alpacas raced through the alleyway between two tearooms. Alfie followed, but as he cleared the alleyway, he rammed into a woman...

OMPH!

...And knocked her off her feet. Roy and I were there in a heartbeat. "I'm so sorry," said Roy, helping her up.

I picked up her walking stick and her clipboard, and helped gather all the junk that had fallen out of her handbag. "What's the big idea?" she said in a grouchy voice.

It was Mrs. Nethercote. She's always grouchy and this accident hadn't improved her attitude at all. "These hideous animals shouldn't be allowed in the village," she said.

"We're so sorry," said Roy. "We were having a race."

"A race? How careless!"

"We're on our way to the Model Village."

Mrs. Nethercote squinted her mean eyes at us. "Why would you go to the Model Village? Only visitors go there."

Roy said, "It's part of our investigation. We think something weird is going on over there."

"Rubbish," said Mrs. Nethercote. "I've never heard of anything so ridiculous. I suggest you and these hideous llamas go home and stay put."

People often mistake alpacas for llamas, but even though they're similar, they're very different. The same is true with dinosaurs. My Mom, for example, doesn't know a microceratops from a dilophosaurus, even though it's really easy to tell them apart. And every time I explain it to her, she says, "Okay, fine, whatever."

Roy set Mrs. Nethercote straight. "They're not llamas, they're alpacas. They're special."

"What's so special about them?"

Roy told her how valuable their fleece is and how they can smell amazing things that we fugles can't.

"Really? How fascinating. NOW GO!" snapped Mrs. Nethercote, making a gesture for us to be on our way. So Roy and the alpacas headed off towards the River Windrush. I walked beside Alfie and rubbed his sore head. Then I looked over at Mrs. Nethercote again. She just glared at me - then she scratched her right ear and tugged her chin.

Just then, Alfie lost his balance and fell over, SPLASH, right into the river!

"Whoa, Alfie!" I jumped in the river and helped the frightened sheep get back to dry land.

Roy came back and said, "What happened?" Alfie blinked his eyes and shook himself dry. Water flew everywhere!

As Roy helped Alfie, I looked over and saw Mrs. Nethercote in the distance. She was watching us and, for the first time ever, I don't think she was grouchy. She was laughing at us. Ha, ha!

What's so funny about being sopping wet?

At the Model Village, Roy and I scraped together our

pocket money to pay for admission. We had to leave the alpacas outside again because of the harsh animal-discrimination rule. Fluff snorted to Roy, which was his way of telling Roy to be sure to sniff around the doorways. "Fluff says that's a good way to tell if someone has just come or gone."

"Okay, whatever."

The ticket-seller was Miss Too-Tight-Snotty-Breeches and when she saw us she said, really snotty-like, "Oh, you two again?"

Roy smiled and counted out all his coins. He even counted several times to make sure it was all there. "Yes, the Model Village is great," he said, real nice-like. "We can't wait to take some more pictures." He acted very cool because he couldn't say: This is part of our official investigation. You must cooperate or face life in prison! If he had said that, she might have burst her too-tight breeches.

Roy and I walked around the Model Village and, whenever anyone was watching, we acted very cool, very la-di-da. But the minute we were by ourselves, we looked down every chimney, peeked inside windows, and sniffed all the little doorways. Roy snapped pictures with his camera like a crazy movie-star hunter. Click, click, click!

A few minutes later, Miss Too-Tight-Snotty-Breeches came up to us and said, "You must leave now."

Roy looked at his watch. "Why? It isn't time to close yet."

She got all huffy. "Well, you must leave because children must be escorted by their parents."

"We've been here before without our parents. What's the problem?"

Miss Too-Tight-Snotty-Breeches didn't have an answer so she just walked off in a huff.

Roy and I went back to our investigation, although, to be honest, I don't have a clue about how to gather clues. My nose knows nothing. To me, the door just smelled dusty. About a minute later, Miss Too-Tight-Snotty-Breeches returned. "You must leave at once, because your alpacas are causing a disturbance outside."

I looked at Roy and he looked at me. Could this be true? We went over to the exit turnstile, where we could see the alpacas outside. They were noshing on a bush. Man, you could practically see halos over their heads they were such angels. "They aren't causing any problems," said Roy.

Even Miss Too-Tight-Snotty-Breeches could see this. "Yes, well..." So she went back to the ticket kiosk again. Roy rolled his eyes as if to say Gimme a Break!

A few minutes later, Miss Too-Tight-Snotty-Breeches returned for a third time, and by now she was seriously getting on our nerves. "Now what?" said Roy.

She was snottier than ever. "Alpacas aren't even allowed outside. It's a strict policy."

"Since when?"

"Didn't you read the sign?" She took us over to the ticket kiosk and pointed. "No alpacas...whatsoever!" The sign was handwritten and was about a minute old and had just been taped to the wall. Serious!

"Sorry, but those are the rules," she said. At least Miss Too-Tight-Snotty-Breeches gave us back our money and you can be sure I counted every penny to make sure it was all there.

Outside the Model Village, Roy gathered the alpacas and Alfie the sheep. Emily snorted and sneered at Miss Too-Tight-Snotty-Breeches. Roy said Emily didn't like her, said she smelled like trouble. We had crossed the street and were heading back to the Post Office when I looked back and saw Miss Too-Tight-Snotty-Breeches talking to someone. I nudged Roy. "Hey, look! Miss Too-Tight-Snotty-Breeches is talking to that lady."

"Who?"

"Mrs. Nethercote, the grouchy old lady we knocked down."

Even my Dad thinks Mrs. Nethercote is a grouch. She's always causing problems at the Post Office, always complaining. He says the postmen think she's a grouch, too. That's why they gave her a special nickname. "Wanna know what the postmen call her? The Witch-on-the-Water," I said.

We watched the two ladies talk; they looked like they were upset about something. "What do you suppose they're talking about?" I asked Roy.

"Probably swapping recipes," said Roy. "For witches' brew!" Euuuuuu!!!

Chapter Three

ONCE we had left the Model Village, Roy had to go home. "We'll look at these pictures tomorrow at school," he said.

But did that happen? No way. That's because the next day at school everyone felt like they had to stick their zitty noses in our business. Like that gimp Jason. He kept looking over our shoulders, trying to see the pictures on the camera. Finally I had to squash him like a mosquito.

It wasn't until the end of the day, at football practice, that Roy and I finally got a moment to ourselves. Coach Bernie lectured us about focusing on our game, but Roy and I stood behind the team and focused on the pictures instead.

"Pay attention!" shouted Coach Bernie, breathing down our necks.

"Sorry, we're just looking at some pictures," said Roy.

"You'll both be looking at suspension if you don't focus." He took Roy's camera from him. Harsh!

Coach Bernie jawed on and on until the bells at St. Lawrence's church bonged. The coach said, "Okay, lads, time to go. Hurry!"

Roy went to get his camera back, but the coach ran off like there was a fire or something. "Wait! My camera!"

Roy and I ran after him, but there was no way we could keep up. The coach ran like it was a race or something. He lost us when he turned left at the cemetery near St. Lawrence's church. By the time we got down there, he was long gone, but we found Roy's camera lying on the pavement.

Roy checked it out. Not a scratch. But we couldn't help but wonder: where did he go, and why was he in such a hurry?

"Weird," said Roy.

Later, after dinner, I got an email from Roy. It said he found a big clue – proof that little people lived in the Model Village. He told me to come over and check it out.

I asked my Dad if I could go up to Roy's house, so that he could help me with some homework.

But Dad said, "What's the problem? Maybe I can help."

I said, "Nah, it's really a project. It's a project thing."

"What kind of project?"

Good grief, since when is my Dad so interested in my life? I said, "Look, can I just go up there or not?"

Dad said, "I want you to take your mobile phone and to leave me the telephone number for Roy's parents. And I want you back home by eight. Got it?"

"Yes, sir." I got my mobile phone and left the number and then ran out of there before he whipped out a huge contract for me to sign or something.

Up at Hillcote Farm, we went to Roy's bedroom and closed the door (to keep his family out) and opened the window (to let the alpacas in). We were going to look at the pictures Roy had taken at the Model Village, so I turned the monitor towards the window and said, "Can you guys see?"

The animals just blinked their eyes and looked confused.

Then Roy said the same thing in Pacachatter.

Now the animals nodded their heads.

Sometimes they make me feel like I'm from another planet or something.

Then we heard this little, "Baa." It was Alfie. He couldn't see. He's too short. So Roy climbed out of the window, found a crate, and helped Alfie up on the crate so that he could see in the window, too.

I said, "Hurry! It's already seven thirty and I only have until eight o'clock! I'm going to have to leave before we even get started."

So Roy climbed back in through the window and, at long last, he showed me the big clue he had discovered. "Look, in the alley. Do you see it? That could be important."

I didn't see a thing. "What?"

"Right there! A bag of rubbish!"

A bag of rubbish? "Dude, are you for real?" Okay, so there was a small bag of rubbish in the alley. Big deal. Some visitor could have been a litterbug and tossed it there. No way did it prove to me that little people were living there.

He switched to another picture. "Look: there isn't any rubbish in this picture. So what do you think?"

"I think I walked all the way up from the Post Office to Hillcote Farm for nothing," I said.

"But what about what Fluff said – he thinks he saw a little person run into the Model Village. Alfie thinks someone ran under him and tickled him."

I gave Roy a look. "Yeah, but don't forget, this is coming from a sheep that thinks it's an alpaca."

I think I kind of let the air out of Roy's tyres. "Yeah, maybe you're right."

He did his Pacachatter thing with the alpacas, telling them that the mystery they had sniffed wasn't up to snuff.

But Fluff snorted and flicked his head up in the air. Emily

shook her head and hummed and Thumpet made some weird noise, too. They were upset.

"What'd they say?"

"Fluff said the first time we were there it was Zippo Time."

"Zippo Time? What's that?"

"That's Pacachatter for the time of day when things go dark."

"You mean dusk?"

"Yeah. But Fluff said that when we went back it was Moko Time, which is Pacachatter for morning. He thinks we should have gone at five bongs."

"Five bongs?"

"Five o'clock – when St. Lawrence's bongs its bells and the shops close up."

Just then, Alfie started "baa"ing like crazy. Roy laughed. "Alfie says, 'Five bongs is when that man tickled my tummy when he ran underneath me.'"

So Roy and I told the alpacas we'd give this mystery thing one more chance. We'd check out the Model Village tomorrow at five bongs. And, speaking of bongs, I checked my watch. "Yikes! Eight bongs! Gotta go!"

I ran all the way back home to the Post Office. Dad was waiting by the back door with his arms crossed. He had that disappointed look on his face. "I said eight o'clock! You know the rules – no television tonight."

"But 'Doctor Who' is on tonight!"

"Those are the rules."

So I went to my bedroom, closed my door, and watched it online instead.

Shhh! Don't tell my Dad!

Chapter Four

T HE next day in school, our teacher, Mrs. Jenkins, asked Roy, "What book is your book report on?"

Roy stood up, looked over at me, and said, "The name of my book is: Meet Me at the War Memorial at Five Bongs."

Message received loud and clear!

Mrs. Jenkins made a face and said, "Hmmm, interesting title."

So I went to the War Memorial at exactly five bongs and waited and waited but Roy was a no-show.

Did I get the message wrong? Or is there really a book with that title?

Eventually, Roy and the alpacas and, of course, Alfie the sheep showed up, puffing and panting. Roy said that getting out of the house at five bongs was tough. His entire family is expected to be home at that hour for tea, unless Roy is at football practice, and the animals are supposed to be in the barn for the night. But at exactly 4:45 p.m. Roy asked his Mum if she wanted a newspaper.

"No," she said. "Tea will be ready soon."

That wasn't the answer Roy wanted to hear. His Mum always wanted a newspaper. "Are you sure? I don't mind."

"Not tonight, ta."

Roy is a lousy liar, but he said, "But I, uh, need some pencils for school."

Totally lame, right? But his Mum actually bought it. She gave him money for a newspaper and pencils. How lucky is that!?

By the time Roy and the alpacas got to the village, all the shops were closing. Shopkeepers locked up their shops and headed for home. Visitors headed for the car and coach parks. Everyone cleared out. Here one minute, gone the next.

Roy said, "Now that it's Zippo Time, let's look for anything suspicious. You and Emily and Thumpet look to the left side of the street. Fluff, Alfie and I will look to the right. We'll meet you at the other end of the village, by the Old New Inn, in ten minutes." Then he repeated everything in Pacachatter.

So Team Roy headed to the right and Team Bruce stood around because I didn't know what to do. Emily and Thumpet sniffed and snorted and went on without me. They sniffed the rubbish bins. I watched Roy across the street. He looked like a real detective, checking out the alleys and doorways. I figured that was what I should do. I faked it. Totally.

At the other end of the village, near the Old New Inn, I saw the alpacas crane their long necks as if they had heard something. Their ears perked up. Then Alfie started to "baa baa baa" like mad.

We all ran over to the sheep. Roy did his Pacachatter thing with Alfie, and then told me, "Alfie says it tickles every time someone runs underneath him."

Had someone just run under Alfie? Or was he ticklish? Or did this sheep that thinks it's an alpaca just have a big imagination? I wasn't sure.

Still, using his nose, Alfie pointed towards the Model Village!

So Roy and I and the alpacas ran over there, but by the time we got there Miss Too-Tight-Snotty-Breeches was locking it up for the day. When she saw us, she gave us the evil eye.

Roy was determined to peek inside, but a honey-stone wall surrounds the Model Village and it's extremely high. I've never seen the Great Wall of China, but I seriously doubt it has much on the wall that surrounds the Model Village.

Roy said, "We need to see what's going on in the Model Village after hours. Serious."

I looked over to see if Miss Too-Tight-Snotty-Breeches could hear us, but she was gone. What I did see was this jackdaw in a tree up above. I've never seen such a big black bird before and, I swear, it was giving me the evil eye, too.

Roy had to get back up to Hillcote Farm, but first he had to buy some pencils and I was desperate for chewing gum, so we went to the Texaco garage because it's the only place in the village that never closes.

Afterwards, Roy said, "Be thinking of a plan to sneak into the Model Village after hours."

I said, "Sure," and then we went our separate ways. As I walked back home I tried to think of a plan, but it's kind of hard to do that and chew gum at the same time. I'm not kidding. Then I saw a jackdaw fly right above me. It was like a stealth bomber directly overhead! Then I wondered if it really was a jackdaw; maybe it was a vulture!? I'm not too sure what a vulture actually looks like, and I couldn't help but wonder if this bird was sizing me up for dinner. I swallowed my gum! Just as I had totally convinced myself that birdzilla was going to peck my eyes out and leave me to perish, it flew off and landed on the windowsill of this old cottage near Station Road.

The jackdaw actually went inside through a window that was cracked open. How weird, I thought, I've gotta tell Roy about this. And when I walked by the cottage I could see two shadows inside, talking.

I wonder who lives in that creepy old cottage?

I hauled my buns home fast and wrote an email to Roy telling him all about it.

The next day, Roy had the LET'S SNEAK INTO THE MODEL VILLAGE PLAN all planned out and the best part of the plan was that I didn't have to plan any of it.

The plan called for a sleepover at Roy's house. Then, after dinner, we were to sneak out of his house, then sneak into the Model Village and sneak out again without getting caught.

But we soon discovered an unexpected flaw in the plan.

What if dinner never ended?

Man-o-man, that's what it felt like. We sat at the table with Roy's family: his Mum, Dad and teenage sister, Chloe. Even his grandmother, Nan Olga, was there. We figured dinner would only take five minutes, six at the max, but not tonight. No, tonight Roy's Dad had to jaw on and on about his newest gizmo, The Super Sheep Sleep 'n' Fleecer. He was all excited because he had a chance to be on 'The Dragons' Den.' That's a television program where inventors ask millionaires to invest millions in the inventions and then the millionaires laugh and make fun of the stupid inventions and keep all their money. (I figure that's why they're millionaires and the inventors aren't, but I guess Roy's Dad hasn't figured that out yet.) So Roy's Dad said, "Two scouts are coming to the Victorian Late-night Shopping Event and whilst they're here they want to give my invention a look-over. Imagine!"

Well, just the mention of the Victorian Late-night Shopping Event sent Roy's Mum into overtime. She jawed on and on about all the problems she was having – nobody was willing to help this year, blah, blah, blah. "This is the biggest night of the year," she said, "and people are behaving, well, so small!"

"You mean like midgets?" I asked. "...Yeouch!"

Roy kicked me under the table!

Nan Olga told Roy's Mum that she always worries too much, that everything would be just fine, but it was hard to take Nan Olga seriously because she had forgotten to put in her false teeth.

Next, Chloe bored everyone talking about her stupid ballet class. This was the straw that broke the camel's back. I nudged Roy and tapped my watch; he nodded in agreement. So he stood up and said, "Excuse us, but it's way past Bruce's bedtime." He headed for his bedroom.

I was surprised, but I managed a yawn and left the table, too.

Once I was in the bedroom, I shut the door. "My bedtime?"

"Hey, I'm a lousy liar. So sue me."

Whatever.

Roy thought we should double-check our plan to make sure it was flawless. So we went over it again, detail by detail.

1) Sneak out of the house and down into the village without anyone noticing us.

Check.

Sneak into Mr. Notgrove's garden and climb over the back wall into the Model Village.

Check, well...

(Okay, I admit, I saw a flaw in step 2. Mr. Notgrove is seriously old and cranky and I know his hearing is lousy, but what if he had bought a new hearing aid that day, and managed to hear us? He might call the police or – worse – my Dad! But did I say anything to Roy? Well, no.)

Investigate the Model Village after dark. Check for mysterious lights, drawn curtains, any signs of intelligent life.

Check.

(Okay, I saw a flaw in step 3, too. Can't explain it, but to me it's straight out of a science-fiction book.)

Climb back over wall and return to Mr. Notgrove's garden. Do not lose any evidence found in MV investigation.

Check. (Another flaw – see step 2.)

Return to Hillcote Farm without being caught. Pretend nothing ever happened.

Check.

"Okay, is there anything else?" asked Roy. "Anything we forgot?"

"No, the plan is perfect!" I lied.

Okay, so I'm a liar. So sue me!

We crept out of Roy's bedroom window and tiptoed down the hill to a gate. Roy unlatched the gate, but that's when we both heard something. A familiar humming...

"What are you guys doing here?" said Roy.

I turned around and, even though it was dark outside, I could see the alpacas. They were following us. Alfie, too. Roy did his Pacachatter thing with them; then he told me, "They want to come, too, but first we have to get Thumpet."

So, instead of sneaking off, we sneaked back to the barn. It was dark and smelly in there. We found Thumpet lying in a corner, his head hung low. "Are you coming with us, Thumpet?" asked Roy.

Thumpet hummed.

"Why not?"

Another hum.

"There's nothing to be afraid of."

Even though I don't speak Pacachatter I knew exactly where Thumpet was coming from.

Fluff and Emily and Alfie came over. Emily hummed. Roy said, "She said, 'Come on, Thumpet, we're doing this as a herd.'"

Thumpet didn't move.

Then Fluff snorted.

All of a sudden, Thumpet was up on his feet, ready to go.

"What'd Fluff say to change Thumpet's mind?" I asked.

"Fluff said, 'If you stay here alone, a wolf might get you.'"

"That works!"

So Roy and I tiptoed back across Hillcote Farm to the gate, with the alpacas doing their alpaca version of tiptoeing, which is more like tip-padding, behind us. Just as Roy was unlatching the gate for a second time, we heard a voice say, "Going somewhere?"

My heart jumped up to my throat. I saw a shadow behind a tree. "Chloe!"

"Where are you two going?" she asked.

"None of your business," said Roy.

"Well, you have a choice," she said, all bossy-like. "Either give me your pocket money for the next three months, or I tell Mum and Dad. And that goes for you, too, Bruce."

Blackmail! I had never been blackmailed before and, I promise you, it felt lousy.

"How did you know we were out here?" asked Roy.

"No one goes to bed at seven o'clock. Not even twerps like you two."

Another flaw in our plan, and we should have seen it coming!

That's when we heard another voice.

"What's going on out here?" It was Roy's Dad.

Busted. Totally busted! (But, in a weird way, I felt better because, even though I didn't see the flaw in our plan, I felt better knowing Chloe hadn't seen a flaw in her plan either.)

So the blackmail threat was down the toilet. But the sleep-over was down the toilet, too. Roy's Dad sent me home packing.

Man, next time we need to triple-check our plan. There were more flaws than either of us could ever have imagined.

Chapter Five

A COUPLE of days later, at school, Roy handed me a note as I passed him in the hallway. Do you have PLANS for lunch?

I had a hunch lunch was about trading information, not sandwiches.

I was right ... and wrong.

Roy had already planned our next plan. Here are the details:

Skip football practice.

Hide out in Mr. Notgrove's garden.

At five bongs, once the Model Village is closed, climb over wall and investigate.

To me, the plan was airtight and bulletproof. So we shook hands over it and Roy said, "I've got tuna with sweetcorn. What have you got?"

"Peanut butter and jam. Wanna swap?"

So we traded information and sandwiches.

Later that afternoon we were barely five minutes into our plan when we discovered our first flaw. Hiding out in Mr. Notgrove's garden, I took one look at the wall and said, "No way!" We had forgotten how high it is. I said, "We'll need ropes and ladders and maybe even a crane to get over."

"No," said Roy. "We need money."

We went to the First National Bank of Bruce, located in my bedroom, in the top drawer of my dresser, and made a withdrawal. Then we marched back to the Model Village and bought two tickets.

"You two again?" said Miss Too-Tight-Snotty-Breeches. We just smiled, real nice and polite, and then I said, "Don't worry, we didn't bring the alpacas. We're just going to have a look around ... Ow!"

Roy had kicked me again.

Once we were inside and out of earshot of Miss Too-Tight-Snotty-Breeches, Roy told me the new plan. We were supposed to look for a safe place to hide out until the Model Village closed. We also needed to find an escape route for afterwards. "Which do you wanna do? Look for a hideout or an escape route?"

"I'll just follow you," I said.

Roy groaned, but I didn't care. I'm lousy at this investigation stuff. It wasn't long before we found both a hideout and an escape route. (Well, okay, Roy found them.) The hideout was behind the miniature of St. Lawrence's church. And to escape all we needed to do was jump up on top of the little church and climb the steeple; then we could reach the top of the high wall. (If we didn't fall off and kill ourselves, that is!) The tricky part, though, was the top of the wall: it had lots of sharp, pointed rocks to discourage people from climbing over. Certainly discouraged me!

Roy must have noticed my knees shaking, so he changed the plan again. "Okay, I'll do all the stuff inside the Model Village. I want you to go and get some rope and wait for me on the other side – in Mr. Notgrove's garden."

"Sure thing," I said, and my knees agreed.

"When you see me up on top of the wall, throw me the rope and help me down."

"Good plan!" I said, and headed for the exit.

"Wait!" I turned around and Roy said, "My Mum expects me to be home soon, so call her and make something up."

"Like what?"

"I dunno. Tell her that the coach is keeping me after football practice or something."

"Me? You call her!"

"You're a better liar than I am."

Was this a compliment? I agreed but I didn't like it. "Okay," I said, and headed for the exit again.

"Wait!" Roy said. "And say something to Miss Too-Tight-Snotty-Breeches to make her think I've already gone home."

"Like what?" I asked.

"Crikey, do I have to do everything?"

So Roy hid behind the miniature St. Lawrence's church, with his camera at his side, and I left to do all the dirty work. On my way out of the Model Village I saw Miss Too-Tight-Snotty-Breeches over in the ticket kiosk. I waved and was real nice when I yelled, "Bye! Thanks! See ya soon!"

She just gave me the evil eye.

I walked halfway back to the Post Office, but her evil eye had me worried. Did she still think Roy was there? What if she caught him hiding? Roy would blame me for the rest of my life. Maybe longer. No, I couldn't take that chance. I went back.

Miss Too-Tight-Snotty-Breeches was busy counting all the money in the till. "Excuse me," I said. "My friend left before I did, but I didn't see which way he went."

"I didn't see him either," she said, without even bothering to look at me.

Did this mean she thought Roy was still in the Model Village? Or did she believe me but wasn't paying attention? Or was she just faking me out? I'm the worst at this investigation stuff. I said, "So, do you know where he is or not?"

Miss Too-Tight-Snotty-Breeches gave me the evil eye again. "Can't you see I'm busy?"

I did my banana thing: I split.

I went to the car park and hid behind a van and watched as visitors left the Model Village. When the bells of St. Lawrence's church bonged I knew it was five o'clock and time to close. A few minutes later I saw Miss Too-Tight-Snotty-Breeches lock up the place, and then she took some bags to the Old New Inn. I figured she believed me and thought Roy was gone, too. But that meant he was locked inside the Model Village for real, and this made me real nervous because now our plan had to work perfectly! No flaws allowed.

I ran back home to the Post Office and got some rope out of a shed in our garden. Then I phoned Roy's Mum – man, my heart was pounding! – but she didn't answer, so I left a message. What a relief! My parents were busy closing up the Post Office, so it was easy to sneak out and go back over to Mr. Notgrove's garden and hide out behind a big bush by the public footpath.

I waited and waited and it got colder and darker by the minute. Finally, I heard a noise and looked up. Roy was up on top of the wall.

"Throw me the rope!"

I sneaked across Mr. Notgrove's garden and tossed up the rope. But as soon as Roy caught it, I knew I was in trouble. That's because it's a very short rope and a very high wall.

"How am I supposed to get down?"

A flaw in the plan!

Roy jumped and landed next to me with a SERIOUS THUD.

"What's going on out here?" It was Mr. Notgrove, coming out of his house, shaking a fist at us.

I helped Roy to his feet and we made a run for it.

"Stop! Hooligans!"

Roy ran with amazing speed considering he had just crash-landed. I could barely keep up with him. We ran all the way to the Post Office and ducked into the alley. "I saw them!" he said, breathing hard. "They live there!"

"Who?" I was gasping for air, too.

"And they saw me! They were totally freaked out!"

"Who??"

"The little people!"

Chapter Six

I WAS blown away. "Little people? For real?"

Roy nodded. "They live there. They're about this high," he said, his hands measuring about fifteen centimetres. "They all said, 'Go! Get out! Before she catches you.'"

"Who???"

"Mrs. Nethercote!"

I had never seen Roy so wired. Or so scared.

"Did you get any pictures?" I asked.

Roy slapped his forehead. "I forgot!"

"How could you forget?"

"Hey, lay off, I'm just a fugle." Then he looked at his watch. "I've gotta go home." He ran off down the alley, even though I had about a million questions. "Email me!" I shouted.

The next day was Saturday, which means no school – yahoo! – so my idea was to just hang out next to my computer, play a few games and wait for an email from Roy.

Didn't happen.

That's because my Dad had ideas of his own. First, he made me stuff all the Saturday newspapers, which is a total pain! Every newspaper has to have next week's television guide in it, or the people in Bourton go ballistic! *Where's my television guide?"* they whine. *"How am I supposed to know what's on telly?"*

Haven't they discovered the amazing sport called Channel Surfing?

After I had finished stuffing all the stupid newspapers, Dad told me to take a parcel to Mrs. Powell over at the Chit Chat Café. I said, "Okay, but first I gotta check my emails."

"Now!" he said.

At this rate my emails were gonna die of old age before I got to them.

The Chit Chat is a small café. Seriously small. Even the tables and chairs are tiny. I think my Dad sent me over with the parcel because his head bumps the beams in the ceiling.

I gave the parcel to Mrs. Powell, who works there. "Oh, lovely," she said. "I've got the Women's Club coming this morning and I couldn't get to the Post Office today. This is very kind of you. Would you like a cup of tea?"

"No thanks," I said. "I have to get back and check my emails."

"My scones just came out of the oven. Sure you won't stay?"

Then this thought hit me: What if my computer crashed this morning and I can't download emails anyway? "Well, maybe just one," I said.

Mrs. Powell sat me at a tiny table in the kitchen, because she had the dining room all set up for the Women's Club, which is a bunch of old ladies who drink tea and gossip. Once a year they sell calendars and then give all the money to a charity. I wish I were a charity.

So I sat in the kitchen, but I could see out into the dining room and you won't believe who walked in – the Witch-on-the-Water. I'm serious! Mrs. Nethercote.

I crouched low so she couldn't see me. I watched as she took off her coat and used her stick to get around. Mrs. Powell went out and I could hear the ladies perfectly. Mrs. Powell said, "Morning, Mrs. Nethercote. You're here early."

"Early?" said Mrs. Nethercote.

"Aren't you with the Women's Club?" asked Mrs. Powell.

"No. Will the WC be here today?" Mrs. Nethercote looked around the room and it was sooo obvious she knew they were coming. "Well, I shan't be in the way."

"Let me get you some tea," said Mrs. Powell.

"Thank you," said Mrs. Nethercote. "And let's hope it isn't tepid like it was last time."

Mrs. Powell came back into the kitchen, and she had exactly the same sour look on her face as my mother has when she finds my bedroom is a mess.

I had to tell Roy. I always carry my mobile phone with me, but my Dad says: "It's for emergencies only!"

Hey, if a Witch-on-the-Water sighting isn't an emergency, what is?

I phoned Roy and told him where I was and who had just walked in.

"Watch her," he said, "and pay attention to everything she does. Everything! The little people in the Model Village are afraid of her. Find out why. I want a full report."

Man, talk about pressure! Mrs. Powell brought me tea and a scone, which, by the way, was deeee-licious! Still, I kept my eyes glued to Mrs. Nethercote. I watched her run her fingers across several tables, checking for dust and sticky stuff. Then she sat down at a tiny table and looked out the window. She watched a couple on the Coronation Bridge. They were smooching and holding hands and I think all that lovey-dovey stuff was making Mrs. Nethercote sick to her stomach (the couple were so mushy they even made me a little sick!) Then this weird thing happened: Mrs. Nethercote scratched her left ear and rubbed her chin. All of a sudden the couple fell off the bridge and into the river. SPLASH! Just like when Alfie fell into the river. Mrs. Nethercote sat and watched and just laughed and laughed. The couple were soaking wet and in no mood to smooch any more.

Then all the old ladies from the Women's Club showed up. The Chit Chat is small enough, but with all the old ladies and their shopping trolleys and bags and coats and scarves and stuff, man, it was seriously crowded. And noisy! Yak, yak, yak. Mrs. Powell served them all tea and scones and she ran around like someone had pushed Fast Forward on her remote control.

Mrs. Nethercote ignored them all and just stared out the window.

Once the old ladies had had their tea, a nice lady named Mrs. Hyde-Winthrop thanked them all for coming and said, "As you know, the Victorian Late-night Shopping Event is coming up, and it's always a marvellous opportunity to sell calendars. Do I have any volunteers?"

Several old ladies raised their hands.

Mrs. Nethercote frowned. "I hate to interrupt," she said, "but do you really think it's a good idea? Isn't it dangerous to sell calendars outdoors on a cold winter's night?"

"Dangerous?" asked Mrs. Hyde-Winthrop. "How so?"

"Well, accidents happen," said Mrs. Nethercote. "What if someone buys a calendar, then turns around and falls in the river? Or trips and breaks a leg? Do you have insurance?"

Mrs. Hyde-Winthrop smiled and said, "Oh, it's just one evening. Everything will be fine, I'm sure." Lots of old ladies nodded their heads in agreement. "I know you have a petition to stop the event," Mrs. Hyde-Winthrop continued, "but it's such a lovely evening. We enjoy it so, don't we ladies?" Again the old ladies nodded their heads and yak, yak, yakked like crazy.

And then Mrs. Nethercote did it again – I saw it with my own eyes! She scratched her nose and tapped her left shoulder. When Mrs. Hyde-Winthrop sat down in her chair, it collapsed. CRASH! She fell to the floor and knocked over the table behind her. That caused the next table to fall over, too. And the next. Scones everywhere! Teapots flew. Man, it was like a motorway pile-up in the middle of a tearoom!

Mrs. Powell had her hands full: overturned tables, smashed teapots, and hysterical ladies.

Mrs. Nethercote helped Mrs. Hyde-Winthrop to her feet and said, "See, accidents happen."

Mrs. Hyde-Winthrop was so upset. "Yes," she said, "I see now what a terrible idea it was." While the old ladies put the room back together, Mrs. Hyde-Winthrop said, "Ladies, I suggest we cancel our plans for the Victorian Late-night Shopping Event. Another time perhaps."

All the old ladies agreed. Mrs. Nethercote whipped out her petition and shoved it at Mrs. Hyde-Winthrop. She signed it in a flash. I've never seen her so scared. She handed the petition to the other old ladies and they all signed it.

I had so much to tell Roy! I ran out the back door and all the way back to the Post Office. Then I remembered that I had forgotten to thank Mrs. Powell for the scone, but I think she had enough to do finding crash helmets for old ladies so that they could finish drinking their tea.

And it was all thanks to one seriously mean and rotten Witch-on-the-Water!

Chapter Seven

SOMETIMES, I wish I had been struck by lightning, too.
... Wait, forget I said that!

Here's what I really mean: if lightning had struck me then I could speak Pacachatter, too. That would make my life way easier. The way it is now, I say something, then Roy tells the alpacas, and then they say something, and Roy tells me, and back and forth and back and forth. It's like a tennis match with words.

That was what it felt like later that day, when Roy called an important meeting in his bedroom. Wimbledon: Bruce vs. the alpacas.

The meeting began with Roy's report. It was very official, very Roy. He told me that he had seen exactly three small people in the Model Village and that they were about fifteen centimetres tall.

Then Roy told the alpacas the same thing in Pacachatter. (To alpacas, fifteen centimetres is about an ear and a bit.)

Then he told me that one of the little people was Bernie, the Coach of our football team. He told the alpacas the same thing and Alfie bleated something and Roy told me, "Alfie said, 'See, he did run under me. An alpaca always tells the truth.'" (Funny coming from a sheep!)

Another little person Roy saw was Mrs. Higgins. She works

at the grocery store, and every time we go there we wonder what colour her hair will be. Every day it's different. Red, green, purple, you name it. I think it's kinda funny, but my Dad says, "Every day is a Bad Hair Day for Mrs. Higgins." Harsh!

The third small person Roy saw was Amelia, who works for my Dad at the Post Office. "No way!" I said. "How can she be big during the day and small at night?"

"Good question," said Roy. "And how come some people are small and other people aren't?"

"I'm gonna ask Amelia the next time I see her."

"And ask her how come some people are small and others aren't."

Fluff snorted and one ear perked up.

"What'd he say?" I asked.

"Fluff asked, 'What do all these little fugles have in common?'"

We both realized the answer at the same time – they were all afraid of Mrs. Nethercote!

"What is it about the old Witch-on-the-Water that they're afraid of?" asked Roy.

"A million things," I said. "She's ugly, she's mean, and she's the biggest grouch in the village..."

All of a sudden it was like another bolt of lightning had struck Roy's brain. "That's it!" he said. I could see the micro-processor in his brain going into overload. "Maybe she really is a witch!" He went straight to his computer and searched the web.

Fluff and Emily hummed and snorted and their ears stood straight up. So Roy turned his monitor around so that they could see, too.

"Check this out," he said to all of us. It was a website about magic spells and potions and stuff about witchcraft. "According to the website, witches can live for three-hundred years and are prone to warts and pterygium eyes."

"What's that?" I asked. The alpacas snorted, so they wanted to know, too.

Roy googled pterygium eyes. It's a flap of skin growing over the eye. Eu!

Roy went back to the Magic Spells site. He read up about witches who can cast spells, hexes and curses. "I dunno," he said, sounding very doubtful. "Mrs. Nethercote is old, but three hundred? She's just like some of the other grouchy old ladies in the village – I'm not convinced she's a witch."

So I told Roy what had happened at the Chit Chat Café. How Mrs. Nethercote had scratched her nose and pulled her ears and then chairs had collapsed and tables turned over. "Those poor old ladies needed an ambulance just to drink their tea." And then I told him about the couple falling into the river. "The same thing happened to Alfie. The Witch-on-the-Water scratched this and twitched that and suddenly Alfie was doing the backstroke in the river."

Roy told the alpacas what I had said and then scribbled all this information down onto his notepad. "This is important info," he said. The alpacas snorted and stomped their feet. They thought it was important, too. I felt kinda proud.

The alpacas snorted again.

"I agree with Fluff," said Roy. "This calls for a stake-out." Then he got a phone book and looked up A. Nethercote. "Here's her address," he said. "She lives on Station Road. Let's do it tonight."

I wasn't sure a witch stake-out was such a great idea. To me, it's a great idea like jumping off a cliff is a great idea. NOT! So I said, "Well, let's think about this. I mean, if she's a witch and catches us, then she could turn us into toads or something."

Roy laughed. "Don't be ridiculous," he said. "She won't do that. She'll just kill us."

Suddenly, jumping off a cliff seemed like the better idea!

That evening, at dinner, I had to be very clever. I had to get information about Amelia, sneak out of the house by six thirty to join Roy and the alpacas for the stake-out, and figure out a way to make my brussels sprouts disappear without Mom noticing.

"Mmm, dinner is delicious, Mom," I said, to throw her off track. Then I turned to Dad and said, "Oh, by the way, has Amelia ever mentioned that she shrinks at night?"

Dad gave me a funny look. "What is that supposed to mean?"

"Well, someone in the village said that she shrinks every evening, and I was wondering if she had ever mentioned it."

Dad said, "It's just gossip. Pay no attention. I can tell you this - only a small person would say something like that."

Okay, end of that subject. Next, the stake-out. "I think Foggy needs to go out for a walk. Okay?"

Mom said, "Now? In the dark? It's cold out."

"Do you want Foggy to wee in the house?"

Mom and Dad shared one of their What's-He-Up-To? looks. I hate it when they do that.

"Eat your brussels sprouts first."

"I would, but I'm so full. Even though they were so delicious."

"Eat!"

So I had to. Man, I hoped Roy would appreciate all the suffering I had had to go through for this stupid stake-out.

Roy and the alpacas were waiting in front of the Old New Inn and Roy wasn't thrilled to see Foggy. "What'd you bring your dog for?"

"He's my excuse to get out of the house," I said. "Why'd you bring your alpacas and a..." I was about to say sheep, but Alfie gave me a 'don't you dare' look.

"They're part of the stake-out team," said Roy. "Just make sure your dog doesn't bark and make noises."

"Yeah, yeah, whatever." The truth is: I wanted Foggy for protection. If the Witch-on-the-Water tried something funny, I wanted Foggy to attack her. (I just hoped she couldn't turn a dog into a three-headed snake or something.)

So with Roy and me and a dog and three or four alpacas – depending on how you count Alfie – we were one big stake-out team. Roy had Mrs. Nethercote's address and we headed up Station Road. "That's her house over there," he said, pointing, "just beyond the cemetery."

I immediately recognized the cottage and freaked. "That's the cottage where I saw a jackdaw fly in the window."

"It is?" Roy told the alpacas in Pacachatter and Fluff snorted. "He said, 'Blimey. This could be important.'"

A honey-stone wall surrounds Mrs. Nethercote's cottage, with a wooden gate at the end of the path. We checked to see if the gate was open – it was! – and then crept into her garden.

Mrs. Nethercote's cottage reminded me of...well, Mrs. Nethercote. It was old and twisted and scary-looking. There were lights on inside so we figured she was home. The window where a jackdaw flew in was still cracked open and I wondered if other horrible creatures might be in there. If Mrs. Nethercote is a witch, anything is possible.

The alpacas sniffed and snorted and their ears perked up. To me they looked like they were searching for hard evidence. Foggy, on the other hand, took me at my word when I said we were going for a walk. He kept going in the wrong direction. Roy had a heck of a time keeping us all together.

There's a shed at the end of Mrs. Nethercote's garden, and Roy told us to hide behind it. From there we spied on the Witch-on-the-Water. We saw shadows in her cottage; she was talking to someone. We listened. "Wow, she sounds really angry," said Roy.

"Yeah, I wonder who she's talking to?" I said.

"I dunno. Let's get closer. Maybe I can take a picture."

That meant I had to leave Foggy behind, at the shed, so I tied his leash around a big flowerpot to keep him in place. Roy told the alpacas to stay put and keep quiet. Then he and I tiptoed over to Mrs. Nethercote's cottage and crouched below the window that was barely cracked open. We could hear two women. One was Mrs. Nethercote, and she sounded angry. The other woman sounded very scared.

"I'm doing the best I can! I swear," said the frightened woman.

"It's not enough!" snapped Mrs. Nethercote. "We must stop their ridiculous event. Ours came first."

"I'll schedule a meeting straightaway," said the other woman. As I listened, her voice sounded familiar – very familiar. Who is that? I wondered.

Roy and I didn't dare make a noise, but Foggy did. He tugged and pulled and barked – he wanted to be over at the cottage with me. Roy gave me a dirty look: Can't you keep your mutt quiet?

Then we overheard Mrs. Nethercote say, "What was that?"

I froze. So did Roy. We could hear her walk closer to the window. "What's that noise outside?"

I held my breath. So did Roy.

By now the alpacas were misbehaving, too. Fluff and Thumpet and Emily were bouncing up and down. Foggy whined. But I could hear Mrs. Nethercote and she was sniffing! Sniff, sniff, sniff! "Do I smell trouble?"

Suddenly, the outside light burst on.

Roy made a run for it! I ran over to Foggy, but he was all tangled up in his leash, so I unhooked his collar and set him free. "Come on, Foggy! Follow me!"

Foggy did as he was told as I ran straight for the gate. Roy and the alpacas and Alfie were already there. I looked back and saw Mrs. Nethercote standing at her window, waving her stick at us.

"What's going on out there?" she shouted.

"Open the gate!" I said to Roy. "Hurry!"

"I can't," he said. "Look at Thumpet!"

Oh no! Thumpet was stuck! Somehow he had gotten his long neck stuck between the wooden slats in the gate, and now he was tangled up. He was upset - his ears were flat down and he was squealing like crazy. Roy tried to untangle him but ...WHOOSH! A huge jackdaw nosedived us! WHOOSH! It barely missed our heads.

"I'm outta here!" I said. Even though Thumpet's neck was tangled in the gate, it was still possible to open the gate. Foggy and I ran out onto Station Road.

Roy tried again to untangle Thumpet, but the alpaca's long neck was in and out of the gate slats like yarn in a loom. The jackdaw swooped down, then back and forth, and now the Witch-on-the-Water was heading for her door.

"Let's go!" I said.

"I can't leave Thumpet," said Roy.

SWOOSH! The jackdaw swiped Roy's head.

"Come on," I shouted.

With the jackdaw circling back again and the Witch-on-the-Water waving her stick, Roy knew he had to leave.

"I'll be back," he promised Thumpet in Pacachatter.

Thumpet hummed and snorted and squealed some more. He tugged and pulled but couldn't break free.

The jackdaw attacked again. Roy and the other alpacas ran for cover.

I looked back at Thumpet. He looked so frightened, so alone. I had to keep running, though, because the jackdaw was headed straight towards me. It followed us all the way back to the Post Office.

We ducked in the alley. The jackdaw flew back and forth but the alley was too narrow for it to fly into. "What about Thumpet?" I asked, even though I was totally out of breath.

"I'll go back for him as soon as I can," said Roy.

"Will he be safe?" I asked.

"I dunno."

"Are we safe?" I asked, looking for that horrible jackdaw.

"Dunno that either," said Roy. Then he and the alpacas and Alfie ran back up to Hillcote Farm. The jackdaw followed him.

Foggy and I were glad to be back home. But did I feel safe? Not!

The jackdaw flew back and forth

Chapter Eight

THE next morning was Sunday, and that means Put-on-Your-Uncomfortable-Clothes-and-Go-to-Church. But first I had to take a shower, and since there's only one bathroom in the house it's always a mad rush to see who gets there first.

I won and was totally naked and ready to jump in when I heard my Dad shout from downstairs, "Where's Foggy's leash?"

Oh no! The dog leash – how am I going to explain this? I wondered. I opened the door a crack and shouted downstairs: "I, uh, lost it. I'll explain later."

"Explain now!" shouted my Dad.

"Can't. I'm naked!"

"I'm coming up!"

Oh man, it's hard enough coming up with excuses when my clothes are on. But naked?!

Dad barged into the bathroom and I invented a lame story about losing the dog leash, but I promised to find it.

My Dad frowned and said, "Alright. And don't use all the hot water."

Too late! Brrrr...that was one cold shower!

I went to church with my parents and, after the longest sermon in the history of the universe, I told my Dad, "I'm so outta here." He was cool about it.

I took a shortcut back to the Post Office and was surprised to see Roy waiting for me in the alley. He looked bummed. "Thumpet's gone," he said.

"What happened?"

"I dunno." He told me that he had gone back to Mrs. Nethercote's house, only to find that Thumpet was no longer trapped in the gate.

"Did he get out? Did he escape? Do you think she has him? Does she have him locked up?"

"I dunno! What are we gonna do? My parents will freak. I'm in serious trouble. We've got to find him."

I ran upstairs, changed out of my uncomfortable clothes and put on some real clothes, and then left a bogus note for my parents. (Looking 4 leash. Later!) Then Roy and I went back to the Witch-on-the-Water's cottage. Sure enough, the gate was there, but Thumpet wasn't.

"Lucky he escaped," I said.

"Why do you think that?" asked Roy.

"Because he's not here, that's why. What do you think?"

"Look!" said Roy. "The gate is closed. It was open when we left Thumpet here last night. If Thumpet got free, why would he close the gate?"

Man, how did Roy get to be so smart? "So you think the Witch-on-the-Water has him?"

He nodded his head. "Let's find out."

"How? We can't sneak in. It's broad daylight. She'll see us."

"Not if we sneak up from the rear."

I was afraid he was going to say that. Behind Mrs. Nethercote's cottage is the cemetery. To me, her cottage is spooky enough, but now we have to cross the cemetery to sneak onto her property. That's extreme spookiness. Hey, not that I believe in ghosts or anything but, well, what if there are ghosts? What if a ghost wonders what we're doing and starts to investigate us? This investigation stuff is getting spooky!

"I think we should look for Thumpet first," I said. "After all, he has his bright moments. Maybe he did close the gate. He might be hanging out somewhere."

Roy agreed to look for Thumpet, but I could tell he didn't think there was much hope of finding him. We went back to the Post Office and I went up to my bedroom to get a map of Bourton. We divided it in half. I was to look for Thumpet in fields and paddocks on the south side of the village and Roy was to look in the north.

"Let's meet back here in the alley at four o'clock sharp," said Roy.

We went our separate ways to look for Thumpet, only I took Foggy with me because he's such a good hunter. Well, he thinks he is anyway. He's mostly good at hunting squirrels or tennis balls. We'd been looking for about five minutes when we ran into Roy.

"What are you doing here?" he asked. "You're supposed to be looking south."

"Isn't this south?"

Roy pointed in the opposite direction.

"Well, excuuuuuuse me, I'm only a fugle!"

So Foggy and I went the opposite way and we looked and looked and looked. We ran through paddocks, looked around the lakes, and even knocked on a few doors to ask people if they had seen an alpaca on the loose. Nobody had.

At four o'clock Foggy and I went back to the alley at the Post Office. A few minutes later, Roy showed up and the alpacas were with him and, of course, Alfie. Every alpaca except for Thumpet.

"I found these guys," said Roy. "They were out looking for Thumpet, too. But we didn't find him. And I'll bet you didn't either."

"No, sorry," I admitted.

"See, told ya so!" said Roy. "That's because the Witch-on-the-Water has him. I think she's done something horrible to him, just like she did to the little people in the Model Village."

"Why do you think that?"

"Because she's a witch! C'mon, let's go check it out."

So Roy sent the alpacas back up to Hillcote Farm because the last thing he wanted was for the Witch-on-the-Water to get them, too. And I put Foggy back in the house. Then we took the public footpath over to the cemetery behind Mrs. Nethercote's house. Along the way, Roy stopped to pick some hedgerow flowers.

"What are you doing that for?" I asked.

"You'll see."

Like everything else in Bourton, even the cemetery is surrounded by a honey-stone wall. Roy and I entered the cemetery through the front gate. Once I was inside, I realized a wall around the cemetery is a good idea - it hides all the tombstones and graves. Some of the tombstones are so old and crooked it looks like they're ready for a graveyard themselves.

There was a man in the cemetery making a fuss over one of the graves. That's why Roy went to another gravestone and put his flowers in front of it. "These are for you Grampy," he said, loud enough for the man to hear.

"Is this your grandfather's grave?" I asked in a whisper.

"No," Roy whispered back, "but act like it is!"

We stood there for a few minutes, pretending to be real sad and upset about his dead grandad, waiting for the other guy to leave. Finally, he split. "Ready? Let's go," said Roy.

The wall around the cemetery wall isn't nearly as tall as the wall surrounding the Model Village, so when I hoisted Roy up and over, it was easy. "Your turn," he said from the other side.

"How am I supposed to get over?" I asked.

"Climb!"

"Yeah, right. I'm not Spiderman!"

"C'mon, Spidey, you can do it!"

Amazingly, I climbed over. I ripped my blue jeans doing it, but I climbed over.

Roy was already searching for Thumpet. "He's not in the garden shed," he told me.

"Aha!" I said, and Roy turned around. He thought I had found Thumpet, but I had found Foggy's leash.

"Keep quiet!" said Roy. "Let's check the garage."

We tiptoed over to the garage and peeked in a window. It was dark inside and the window was dirty so it was hard to see.

"He's not in there," said Roy. "Do you think she would keep an alpaca in her house?"

"Duh! Of course she would. She's a witch," I said. "She probably has him stuffed in a cauldron and is making a magic potion that calls for three toads, two eyes of newt, and one alpaca."

So we crept over to her house and crouched under a window. "Take a look inside!" Roy said in a whisper.

"Me? You look. He's your alpaca."

"Coward."

I didn't deny it.

Roy peeked in the window and took a picture with his camera.

"See anything?" I asked.

"No," he said, "but maybe the picture will reveal something. Let's check another room."

We tiptoed around the corner of her house, quiet as a...

"Looking for something?"

There she was! The Witch-on-the-Water! Right in front of us. I screamed!

Roy, though, was amazing. He stood up to her and said, "Where is he? Where's Thumpet?"

Mrs. Nethercote said, "What are you talking about?"

"My alpaca. What have you done with him?"

Mrs. Nethercote just glared at both of us. "I know nothing about your llama, or whatever it is. I want both of you trouble-makers to leave...right now!"

"Not until I have Thumpet!"

Mrs. Nethercote bent down to threaten Roy. "Do I have to call the police?"

Roy didn't flinch. "Go ahead. You don't scare me. Even if you are a WITCH!"

Well, that was enough to scare me. I was outta there. I ran down the path to her gate so fast my feet were smoking.

At the gate, I turned around and saw that Roy was right behind me. The Witch-on-the-Water shook her stick at us. "Run!" shouted Roy.

We ran all the way back up to Hillcote Farm. Just before we got there, the alpacas met us in the paddock below. In Pacach-atter they said to Roy, "Hurry! Now it's Alfie!"

We ran to the farm and saw Roy's father nudging Alfie over to the Shed of Invention.

"Come with me, woolly one," said Roy's father. "We've got work to do."

Alfie saw Roy and bleated, "Baaa, baaa." I don't speak Paca-chatter but I could definitely understand Alfie. It was "Help me!"

Roy and I and the alpacas stood outside the Shed of Inven-tion and peeked in the window to watch Roy's Dad as he tested his Super Sheep Sleep 'n' Fleecer on Alfie. The poor sheep was strapped to a table, with a headset covering his ears. He looked totally scared. Roy's Dad wore goggles and turned dials and punched gadgets on his machine. Suddenly, lights flashed and sparks flew. It was just like watching a horror movie, starring Roy's Dad as The Mad Gizmo-monger and Alfie as The Sheep of Frankenstein!

"Your Dad is torturing poor Alfie!"

"No," said Roy, "it's just a gizmo to make Alfie sleep. It doesn't hurt." He didn't look convinced, though. "At least, I hope it doesn't."

Alfie was wired. For a sheep that was supposed to sleep, well - I've never seen a sheep look more AWAKE. Even his fleece was standing to attention!

I couldn't bear to watch any more; I turned away from the window. So did the alpacas. They snorted and squealed and flicked their heads up in the air.

It was torture for Roy, too. Finally, he barged into the Shed of Invention and yelled, "Stop! Enough! I'll tell you everything!"

Later, in the house, I ate biscuits and drank a glass of milk while Roy had a total meltdown. He told his parents everything: how Thumpet was missing; about our investigation; about seeing little people at the Model Village; and about Mrs. Nethercote being a witch.

Roy's parents were upset, but for all the wrong reasons. Roy's Dad said, "Let's call the police."

Roy's mother, though, said, "I'm calling a doctor, that's who I'm calling." She was very upset. "Witches, small people, and now the alpaca is missing. This isn't normal! We should have called a doctor long ago."

Roy's Dad turned to me and said, "Bruce, do you know where the alpaca is?"

"No," I said. "We've looked everywhere."

"Have you seen any little people at the Model Village?"

"Well...no."

Alfie was wired

The Super Sheep Sleep 'n' Fleecer

"What about Mrs. Nethercote? Do you think she's a witch, too?"

"Well...I dunno."

"Come on, I'll give you a ride home," said Roy's Dad.

Roy was upset and he ran straight to his bedroom. He didn't say goodbye. He wouldn't even look at me. Nothing.

I felt terrible. It was a long, long, long ride home.

Chapter Nine

MY Mother says, "Everyone likes a compliment now and then," but today, when our teacher, Mrs. Jenkins, gave Roy a compliment in class, man, he got all bent out of shape.

Here's what happened – Mrs. Jenkins gave us an assignment: to write a paper about a discovery we had made. The discovery I wrote about was when I moved from the United States to England. On the plane flying over, I discovered puke bags. They were in the pocket of the seat in front of me. Every time the plane bumped, I had to reach for another bag. I used both of my bags and both of my mother's bags and even the bags that should have been for the nice old lady sitting next to me. Good thing she didn't have to hurl because there weren't any bags left.

Mrs. Jenkins wrote on my paper: "Good report, but the details were not necessary."

I'm telling you, those puke bags were necessary!

Roy's was about what he had discovered at the Model Village. Mrs. Jenkins liked it so much she read it out loud: "Class, listen to this: Roy thinks the Model Village is small because small people live there. My, what a BIG imagination!"

Everyone laughed. Mrs. Jenkins laughed. Even I laughed. Everyone laughed except for Roy. He was upset that Mrs. Jenkins didn't believe his discovery. "It's true," he said. "There are small people living in the Model Village. I'm not making it up. Coach Bernie lives there. I saw him. If you don't believe me, ask Bruce."

Suddenly everyone in class stared at me. I was soooo embarrassed!

"Really, Bruce? Have you seen these small people, too?"

I wish there had been a puke bag on the seat in front of me. I needed one! I think I said, "I dunno."

"Either you have or you haven't."

"Well, I haven't exactly seen them," I confessed.

Roy just glared at me. Man, if his eyes could shoot laser beams, I would have been toast! I've never seen him so upset. Then he stopped looking at me altogether.

For the rest of the day!

After school, I waited outside for Roy, but he walked right past me.

"Hey, did anyone find Thumpet yet?" I asked.

He just kept walking.

"Are you mad at me?" I had to run to keep up with him.

"Duh!"

"What'd I do?"

Finally, Roy stopped and glared at me. "You didn't defend me. You let everyone laugh at me like it's some big joke. Nobody believes what we discovered. Not even you!"

"What do you want me to do - lie? I haven't seen any small people."

"But do you believe I did?"

"Well, I dunno. You said you did."

Roy just walked off. He didn't say another word to me.

For the next two days, I felt invisible. As if I wasn't even there. In class Roy wouldn't speak to me or even look at me. After school, I went up to Hillcote Farm and knocked on the door, but he wouldn't open it.

Just in case Roy was in the barn, I checked there. I found the alpacas, but not Roy. The alpacas hummed and their ears perked up and they seemed glad to see me. I was glad to see them, but it's hard because I don't speak Pacachatter. My big surprise, though, was when I saw...

"Alfie? Is that you?"

Poor Alfie. He had enough problems in life, what with being a confused sheep who thinks he's an alpaca and all. Now he even looked confused. Roy's Dad had finished experimenting with him in the Shed of Invention, and Alfie looked half-sheared and half-scared. What fleece he had left was standing straight on end. Talk about steel wool! I felt sorry for him, so I gave him a doggy treat from my pocket. He liked it, but now he's probably more confused than before – a sheep who thinks he's an alpaca or perhaps a dog.

I said 'later-gators' to the alpacas and went back home. I emailed Roy a couple more times.

Nothing came back.

Even though my Dad only wants me to use my mobile phone for emergencies, I used it to call Roy. It felt like an emergency to me. So what if Dad blows like a volcano.

Voicemail. I didn't leave a message. What's the point? I was invisible.

I never realized all the fun times I had with Roy until the fun times were over. I might never have fun again. Ever in my whole life.

Like the fun times we had in Birdland. It's a big attraction in Bourton-on-the-Water where about a million different types of birds from all over the planet live. Okay, it's kinda sad that they have to live in cages, but at least they get to hang out with all their feathered friends. Visitors love to go there and so do Roy and I. Especially at two o'clock in the afternoon, because that's when the Bucket Man feeds the baby penguins. They yap and squeal and stand on their little feet until the Bucket Man throws them a fish. One time Roy yapped and squealed and was totally surprised when the Bucket Man threw him a fish, too. What a riot!

Another fun time was at the Motor Museum. It's another attraction here in Bourton, with lots of amazing old cars. Roy and I like to go there because it's a chance to goof on people. One of our favourite goofs is to stand next to this old car called Brum and to pretend we're wax figures. When visitors step up close we blink our eyes and they freak! Then we laugh and laugh until the manager asks us to leave.

Then we would go to the Model Railway and ask visitors: "Hey, when's the next train to Cheltenham?" As if! It's nothing but miniature trains.

Going to the Dragonfly Maze was always amazing. A-maz-ing! Get it? It's a really cool maze where people pay to get lost. Seriously! Our favourite goof was to pretend that Roy's sister was still lost in there. We'd tell visitors about to go in that if they found Roy's sister to tell her to come home. "She's been lost in there for three weeks now!" It freaked out a few people. A-maze-ing!

And it was always fun to go to the Perfumery and goof that our noses were broken – "Nope, can't smell a thing!"

Even the witch stake-out a few days ago was fun. It seemed scary at the time, but now, looking back, it was fun just listening to the two ladies, trying to overhear what they were talking about...

Oh my gosh, that voice! Suddenly, I remembered. I know who that voice belongs to! I ran to my computer and wrote an email to Roy: "I know who the Witch-on-the-Water was talking to! I remember! Call or email me." I clicked send.

Then I sent a second email. "P.S. I believe you."

Every Wednesday evening I have to help my Dad close up the Post Office. He's extra busy on Wednesdays because he has to balance books or something weird like that, so my job is to bundle up leftover newspapers and put them in the alley to be picked up the next morning. I was dragging a bundle into the alley, when suddenly I heard, "Meet me at Mr. Notgrove's garden at six thirty."

"Roy!"

He was hiding out in the alley. "Do you need some help?"

Roy said this because I had dropped the newspapers on my toes.

"No, it's okay," I said. Ow, my toes!!!

"Okay, meet me there at six thirty?"

"Sure," I said.

Roy started to walk off again, but I said, "Hey, I know who Mrs. Nethercote was talking to."

"I figured it out, too," he said. "Don't be late!" And then he was gone.

I stood in the alley, rubbing my sore toes, but I didn't care how much they hurt because I was so happy to see Roy. I never knew pain could feel so good.

Chapter Ten

I SCOFFED down dinner in record time and at six twenty-five I told my parents, "Foggy needs to go for a walk."

"It's cold outside. Bundle up. Don't be out long."

"Yeah, yeah, yeah."

"And don't lose his leash," warned my Dad.

"Yeah, yeah, yeah."

Foggy and I left the house and ran to the public footpath behind Mr. Notgrove's house. It was really dark out but I could see Roy. Well, I saw a shadow with rope slung over its shoulder, so I just figured.

"I want you to help me up on the wall and then throw me the rope," Roy said in a whisper – just in case Mr. Notgrove had bought himself a new hearing aid and had the volume cranked to HIGH. "Once I tie it tight then I'll lower it down so you can climb up."

"Me? You want me to sneak into the Model Village, too?"

"Duh! We both need to see this. I need an eyewitness."

No way, I thought. I'd rather shut my eyes than be an eyewitness. "Gee, I'd really love to," I lied, "but I, uh, can't leave Foggy here by himself."

"Yes you can. Tie him to a post. He'll be fine. Let's go!"

Why is it impossible for me to say no to Roy? I tied Foggy to the fence and promised him I'd be right back. He gave me a lick.

At the wall, I cupped my hand and hoisted Roy up so he could reach the top.

"Higher!"

Man, he was heavy! I pushed with all my might. He reached for the top...

CRASH! I collapsed and we both fell to the ground. Foggy barked.

"Shhh! Quiet, boy!" I looked to see if we had disturbed Mr. Notgrove. Either he's stone deaf or he bought a lousy hearing aid, I thought.

Roy and I gave it another try. This time I pushed harder and Roy reached higher and this time he made it to the top. Wasn't long before he tossed down the rope and said, "Your turn. Climb up!"

I tried to think of as many excuses as I could NOT to climb up: I'm not strong enough... I'm scared of heights... What about rope burn??? But, by that time, I had actually climbed to the top! Hey, it was way easier than I thought. We climbed down onto the roof of the miniature St. Lawrence's church and...

We had sneaked into the Model Village!

Roy and I tiptoed over to the miniature Perfumery. (Weird, because it doesn't smell at all. Maybe my nose is broken???) We hid behind it, but by peeking over the top, we had a perfect view of the miniature village green. We didn't move; we remained perfectly still. The only thing I could hear was my heartbeat.

There were lights on in the miniature village. Curtains were drawn. It felt just like Bourton-on-the-Water – only smaller. But, in a weird way, alive.

Roy nudged me and said, "Look! Behind the gift shop!"

That's when I saw the most amazing thing – a little woman walked down a tiny alley and headed for the green. I mean, little! Small. Tiny. She was only fifteen centimetres high!

"Shhhh!" said Roy.

I guess I had gasped. I couldn't help it. It was amazing. I had never seen anything like it. Wow, I'm an honest-to-goodness-genuine-for-real eyewitness, I thought.

Soon other little people joined her. I recognized a few of them. One was Mrs. Higgins, the lady who works at the grocery shop, whose hair is a different colour every day. (Today it was purple). I saw Coach Bernie. And Amelia. I whispered to Roy, "How can Amelia be so big during the day at the Post Office, but so small at night?"

Roy shrugged. "That's what we have to find out."

More little people came out of their little cottages and everyone gathered on the little green, even a little man rolling himself in a little wheelchair. Both of his legs were set in casts. Roy snapped pictures with his camera. Then I noticed two jackdaws overhead; they landed on top of the miniature Victoria Hall. It was kinda creepy because, in the Model Village, where everything is small, these two black birds seemed positively HUGE.

Roy and I did our best to spy on the little people gathered on the green. We could hear Mrs. Wiggins. She seemed real upset. Wringing her hands, she said, "Oh dear, oh dear, this is trouble. I just know it's trouble."

Amelia tried to calm her down. "Now, now, you don't know that."

"Of course it's trouble. Any time that woman calls a meeting like this, it's trouble. I shudder to think."

I looked over at the Victoria Hall, but the two jackdaws were gone. When did they fly off? I wondered. Then, from the back, near the ticket kiosk, I saw two women walk into the Model Village. It was difficult to see in the dark, but they looked like giants compared to the little people standing on the green. One was hobbling with a stick, and the other one was fat and her breeches were too tight.

The Witch-on-the-Water and Miss Too-Tight-Snotty-Breeches!

"That's who the Witch-on-the-Water was talking to at her house," I whispered to Roy.

"I know...shhh!"

The Witch-on-the-Water leaned against her stick and glared at the little people gathered on the green. Then she sniffed. "Who's missing? Someone's missing!"

Miss Too-Tight-Snotty-Breeches did a quick head count. "Everyone's here, I believe. No, wait, we're missing one..."

"Coming! I'm coming," shouted a tiny little lady running down the tiny little High Street.

I nudged Roy. "That's Mrs. Hyde-Winthrop," I said. "She's the lady I told you about at the Chit Chat Café."

"Shhhh!"

The Witch-on-the-Water wagged her finger at Mrs. Hyde-Winthrop when the little woman finally arrived. "Do you know what happened to the last person who was late?"

Little Mrs. Hyde-Winthrop shook her head. "No."

"Tell her, Mr. Peterson," said the Witch-on-the-Water.

Mr. Peterson, the little man in the little wheelchair, pointed to the casts on his legs.

I gasped.

So did Mrs. Hyde-Winthrop. She got the message loud and clear. Everyone did!

"It's cold and damp, so I shan't keep you long," said the Witch-on-the-Water, bundling her coat tighter. "I've gathered you here because the Victorian Late-night Shopping Event is still on schedule, even though I made it perfectly clear that this event must not happen."

All the little people held their heads low, just like puppies being scolded.

Mrs. Higgins was the only one brave enough to speak. "I've

tried but, well, I'm just one little person – especially these days...tee hee hee."

The Witch-on-the-Water picked her up by the back of her coat. "Find that amusing, do you?"

Mrs. Higgins trembled so much her purple wig fell off. The Witch-on-the-Water put her back down again and poor Mrs. Higgins scrambled to put her hair back on.

Mrs. Hyde-Winthrop said, "Sorry, but I'm new to this little group. Am I to understand that you want the shopping event cancelled because you have something planned for the same evening? Is that correct?"

"Not me," said the Witch-on-the-Water. "The Council of Merlin. It's the Night of the Jackdaws, and every witch, warlock and wizard from the council is flying in for the installation of officers. It's a very important night."

"Perhaps your group could relocate to Notgrove? Or Little Rissington? Those are lovely places, too."

"Absolutely not. We've been on the calendar for nearly two-hundred years. Why should we move? We claimed the village green first!"

Mrs. Hyde-Winthrop disappeared back into the little crowd. Then Amelia stepped forward. "My boss has asked me to work that evening. I can't tell him no."

I listened real closely because this was my Dad she was talking about! The Witch-on-the-Water just glared at Amelia and said, "And why not?"

"Because he's been very good to me. I wouldn't want to let him down."

"Do it anyway!"

Amelia was so brave. She stood right up to the mean old Witch-on-the-Water. "Well, I'm not so sure your event would be good for the village. I've heard some disturbing things. Is it true a sheep will be sacrificed?"

"No, of course not," said the Witch-on-the-Water. "Where did you hear such nonsense?" She turned to Miss Too-Tight-Snotty Breeches. "Talonie, fetch our little token and show them."

Miss Too-Tight-Snotty-Breeches left, but Amelia continued. "Still, I think I'm speaking for others when I say that I don't think this Night of the Jackdaws – or whatever it is – is appropriate for this village. Perhaps you should consider moving your event elsewhere."

The little people behind Amelia applauded. But this only made the Witch-on-the-Water red hot with anger. "Oh, really? Is that what you think? Well, you know what I think?"

The Witch-on-the-Water picked up Amelia by the back of her jacket and sniffed her; poor Amelia dangled in mid-air.

"Do I smell a rat?" said the Witch-on-the-Water. Then she scratched one ear and rubbed her eye.

Wow, what happened next was amazing. Unbelievable. Amelia turned into a rat! Right before our very eyes.

The little crowd gasped. So did I.

The Witch-on-the-Water dropped the rat and it scurried away, running off into the night. "Do I smell any more rats amongst you?"

The little crowd gathered closer. Miss Too-Tight-Snotty Breeches returned, carrying a small cage. "Ah, thank you, Talonie," said the Witch-on-the-Water. "Show them our little sacrifice for the event. Let them see for themselves that it isn't a sheep."

Miss Too-Tight-Snotty-Breeches opened the cage and pulled a small animal out by its neck.

Thumpet! The poor little alpaca was no more than twelve centimetres tall. He had been downsized, too.

Roy freaked! He made a noise and suddenly all the small people on the green turned their heads.

"What was that?" said the Witch-on-the-Water, her creepy eyes looking about.

Miss Too-Tight-Snotty-Breeches started to sniff.

"What do you smell?" said the Witch-on-the-Water. "More rats?"

Sniff, sniff. Sniff, sniff.

"This meeting is adjourned," said the Witch-on-the-Water, and she stuffed poor little Thumpet back into the cage and carried it away. The little people scattered. Everyone was frightened.

So were Roy and I. Miss Too-Tight-Snotty-Breeches continued to sniff as she made her way towards us. Roy shoved his camera back in his pocket and we scrambled as fast as we could over to the miniature St. Lawrence's church. We climbed up on its roof and after a big leap we were on top of the wall that surrounded the Model Village. It was going to be a long fall, but neither of us cared. We both jumped!

OMPH! We hit the ground hard.

"Who goes there?"

I looked up and saw mean old Mr. Notgrove shaking his fist at me again.

"Mildred, call the police!" he said.

We made a run for it. I don't know how - because all of my bones were crushed - but I ran all the way back home. So did Roy.

Once I was back home, I soaked my bones, or what was left of them, in a hot bath. Then I went to bed with the light on.

Chapter Eleven

THE next morning, everything hurt. Man, that fall was brutal! I wanted to stay in bed all day. That was until I heard my Dad shout up the stairs, "Where's Foggy? Has anyone seen the dog?"

OH-MY-GOSH!!!!

I've never put on my clothes so fast. I crept out the back door and sped like a bullet back to Mr. Notgrove's garden.

"Foggy!"

I was soooooooo glad to see him. The poor dog had been tied up all night, left alone, out in the cold. But was he mad at me? Did he scold me? No, he gave me doggy licks. And lots of them.

All those doggy kisses, of course, made me feel even worse. I wasn't worthy. I was so caught up in all the Witch-on-the-Water stuff that I kinda sorta forgot. It's a wonder Mr. Notgrove didn't find Foggy or – worse – that the Witch-on-the-Water didn't find him and shrink him, too.

I took my favourite pup on a good walk home. He could lead. Anything he wanted. He deserved it. Foggy rules!

That day in school Roy and I passed notes in the hallway. Roy's note – Now do you believe me?

My note – Duh!

His next note – Mission: Rescue Thumpet! Are you in?

My note back – Major duh! Let's talk @ lunch.

I don't know what Roy's next note was because that gimp named Jason snatched it from me and gave it to our teacher, Mrs. Jenkins, who tore it up and threw it away. How rude!

Even at lunch, Jason was hanging around, trying to listen to what we were saying, until I gave him my sandwich and told him to disappear. Such a gimp!

Once he was gone, we could finally talk and, believe me, there was a lot to talk about.

"How did the Witch-on-the-Water get Thumpet to shrink?" I asked.

"How did she get all those people to shrink?" asked Roy.

"Yeah, and how come some people shrink and others don't?"

"And how come they're big by day, but small by night?"

"Do you think Amelia is stuck being a rat for the rest of her life?" I asked.

"I dunno," said Roy. "What about the Witch-on-the-Water? Is she an old woman, a witch, or a jackdaw?"

"Or all of the above?"

Just then I looked over my shoulder and that gimp Jason was back again. "Do you want me to squash you like a bug?" I said.

The gimp got the message and split.

Roy said, "Okay, so how do we rescue Thumpet?"

"We've got to be careful," I said. "What happens if the Witch-on-the-Water catches us? Will we shrink, too? Or turn into rats?"

Once again, I could feel Jason behind me, eavesdropping. "Beat it, gimp!" I said.

"Ahem!"

I turned around and was surprised to see my teacher, Mrs. Jenkins.

"You're late for class!"

I looked at my watch. Oops. It's like lunch had been set on warp speed.

"To be continued," Roy told me. And we were outta there.

Do you think that gimp Jason ratted us out?

After school, Roy and I had football practice. Coach Bernie drilled the team, but I had to hand it to Roy – he drilled the coach just as hard.

"How does it work? How come you're BIG now, but small at the Model Village?"

Bernie blew his whistle as if Roy had committed a foul or something. "Quiet! Not here, not now!"

But Roy didn't stop. "You've got to tell me. How does it happen? Is it a spell? Does Mrs. Nethercote have total control?"

Coach Bernie pulled Roy aside and looked around to make sure no one was listening. "Don't ask," he said. "Leave things alone. Mind your own business. She's dangerous!"

"She has my alpaca," said Roy. "That makes it my business."

"If you don't stop, she'll come after you, too," warned the Coach. "You have no idea what she's capable of."

When practice was over everyone went home - except for Roy and me. We went to the office and found Coach putting away the sports equipment.

"So, Coach, how come some people are small and others aren't? How does that work? Is it like a club you sign up for or something?"

Again, Coach Bernie looked around to make sure that nobody else could overhear. "Don't be ridiculous," he whispered. "Who would want to join such a club? We live in fear of that horrible woman."

"So it's all up to her? To Mrs. Nethercote?" asked Roy. "She decides who's small and who isn't?"

"Yes...no...go home!"

But Roy pressed on. "Why did she choose you?"

"Go away! Don't ask."

"Why?"

I've never seen Coach look scared before but, believe me, he was. "Because she smells fear," he said, very quietly, "and once she smells your fear, she knows she's got you."

Just then, the bells at St. Lawrence's church started to bong, announcing to the world that it was five o'clock. Coach jumped when he heard the bells and headed for the door. "I've got to go," he said.

"Wait!" shouted Roy. "I have more questions."

But Coach ran as if his life depended on it. Roy and I ran after him, all the way down the footpath to St. Lawrence's church. Coach turned the corner and we could no longer see him because he was hidden behind hedges. When Roy and I eventually got to the church, we could see the Coach again, but he had shrunk. He was still running but he was no more than fifteen centimetres high.

"Coach, wait!" I shouted, running to catch him.

"Look out!" Roy shouted at me. I looked up and saw a jackdaw in the sky. It swooped down, nearly hitting me. I ducked (and I think I might have screamed). Anyway, with its claws the jackdaw plucked up the coach and flew off towards the Model Village. Poor little Coach dangled in the air, in the grip of a horrible black jackdaw.

Man, it gave us the creeps!

Roy and I both agreed to an urgent meeting in his bedroom up at Hillcote Farm. Seven p.m. sharp!

Next came the hard part – getting out of my house.

"Dad, can I go up to Roy's house tonight? It's important, okay? Really important."

"Why can't Roy come down here?" asked my Dad.

"Because..."

"Because why?"

"Because, well, I dunno. Because I'm supposed to go up there, that's why. That's the plan."

My Dad said, "Well, I don't like you out at night, but if it's so important, Roy is welcome to come down here."

Now what was I supposed to do? "Fine," I said, "Roy and the alpacas will be here at seven."

"The alpacas?"

I explained to my Dad that Roy never goes anywhere without the alpacas. He kinda scrunched his face. "Alright, go! But be back home by eight...or else!"

I hate to admit it, but even my Dad has animal-discrimination rules for the house. He only bends those rules for Foggy. Good thing I'm not an alpaca, because he wouldn't even allow me in the house!

So I blazed a trail up to Hillcote Farm. We closed the door to Roy's bedroom to keep his parents out, but opened the window to let the alpacas in. Well, their heads were in, anyway. Alfie stood on a crate in order to see through the window, too.

Our important meeting began. We had a lot to figure out. How do we rescue Thumpet? Could we help the little people? Should we tell the police? Would the police even believe us? And my big question was: "What happens if the Witch-on-the-Water catches us?"

Roy worried about that, too. But he was thinking of other stuff too, like, what happens if we touch Thumpet and then we shrink because this witchcraft stuff is contagious? Wow! Those thoughts never land here on Planet Bruce. And those thoughts freaked me out, too.

We surfed the Internet, searching for info on witches. So much info! Is someone born a witch, or is it a lifestyle choice?

Are there good witches and bad witches? How powerful is a witch? Are spells permanent or reversible? Can witches really ride a broomstick, or have they switched to Smart Cars? We learned a ton.

Here's what Roy found so interesting: there was a blog that said wicked witches prey on the weak and vulnerable. So that kind of went along with what Coach Bernie told us when he said: "She can smell fear." If witches know you're afraid of them, that's when they come after you. Yikes! But wait, here's the cool part – do you know what witches fear the most? (Drum roll, please.........) They fear becoming weak and vulnerable. That means that if they become scared or afraid or wimpy then they lose all their powers.

We also googled all the contagious stuff. We found out that a spell isn't contagious, but that a witch's wart is. Go figure.

Roy translated all of this info into Pacachatter and the alpacas nodded their heads and snorted. He told me, "The alpacas are worried about Thumpet. He's always been weak. He's afraid of his own shadow. They're worried because it's not good to be separated from the herd for such a long time."

Roy said something back to them and they hummed in unison.

"What'd you say?" I asked.

"I told them not to worry. That we'll rescue Thumpet. We're not afraid of witches."

Wanna bet? But I kept that thought to myself.

I got home at exactly seven fifty-nine, but my Dad was sound asleep in front of the television. I woke him up and said, "Look, I'm home!"

"Good," he said, and closed his eyes again.

Man, why couldn't he have been asleep last time when I was late? Not fair!!!!!

Chapter Twelve

MY Mom always says, "Growing up is tough these days." She may be right, but what happens if we grow down? Sometimes I'm not sure if I'm growing up or growing down. Am I big? Or am I small? It's so confusing.

The next day was the worst day of my life because it's the day I officially became a small person.

Well, kinda sorta. Here's what went down.

In the hallway at school, every time I passed Roy he handed me a note. One after another: Meet me here; meet me there; let's do this; let's do that. All the notes were about Mission: Rescue Thumpet.

The more notes he passed, the less I wanted to do it.

Okay, Thumpet deserved to be rescued, but the more I thought about it, the more I thought we should send in the Army. They're good at rescues. Why me?

I've got better things to do than breaking and entering the Model Village, battling witches, kidnapping a shrunken alpaca, and crushing all my bones again after another fall off the Great Wall of the Model Village.

Does this mean I'm a rotten person? Does this make me small?

After school, I met Roy by the football field. Fluff, Emily and Alfie the sheep were there and ready to go.

Roy said, "Mission: Rescue Thumpet begins at Mr. Notgrove's at exactly five bongs. Are you in?"

I don't remember saying anything.

"What's the matter?"

I don't remember answering that one either.

"Don't you wanna help?"

Nothing.

"Are you afraid?"

That was it in a nutshell. But I couldn't admit that to my best friend who needed my help. "No," I lied. "I just don't wanna sneak into the Model Village again. I'm not a criminal."

I figured Roy would whack me in the arm, but he didn't. To my surprise, he said, "You know what, you're right. We're not criminals. They are!"

And he walked off.

"Wait! What'd I say?" It was all I could do to keep up with Roy and the alpacas. He put the alpacas in the garden behind the Post Office. Then I followed him over to the Model Village, where he walked over to the ticket counter and slapped his money down. "We'd each like a ticket, please."

Miss Too-Tight-Snotty-Breeches gave Roy his ticket, and then turned to me. "That will be two pounds seventy-five."

"I'm a little short," I confessed.

"How much short?" asked Miss Too-Tight-Snotty-Breeches.

"Well, two pounds seventy-five. Can I owe you?"

Roy turned to me and said, "Don't you have any money?"

I showed him my empty pockets. Miss Too-Tight-Snotty-Breeches gave us the evil eye again.

Roy said, "Okay, whatever. Wait here. I'll be right back."

Roy left and Miss Too-Tight-Snotty-Breeches glared at me the whole time.

From where I stood, I could see Roy as he looked around the Model Village. He looked high and low for Thumpet, although, let's face it, in the Model Village nothing is very high. He couldn't find the small alpaca anywhere, and I could tell he was ticked off. He came back to the ticket kiosk and said, "Where is he?"

Miss Too-Tight-Snotty-Breeches said, "Where is who?" as if she didn't know a thing.

"Thumpet. My alpaca. I know he's here. We saw him." Roy turned to me. "Didn't we?"

I kinda nodded my head.

Miss Too-Tight-Snotty-Breeches pointed to the No Alpacas sign taped to the ticket kiosk. "Don't be ridiculous. If we don't allow alpacas outside, why would we allow them inside?"

I could almost see steam coming out of Roy's ears. "You've got him here, I know you have! We saw him. I took pictures!" He ran back into the Model Village and shouted to all the visitors: "Listen up, everyone! If anyone sees a little alpaca, please tell me. The Model Village is holding him hostage! I'm not kidding!"

Miss Too-Tight-Snotty-Breeches shot out of the ticket kiosk like a red-hot cannonball. "Stop this at once," she shouted to Roy, "or I'll phone the police."

Uh oh! Roy had caused quite a ruckus in the Model Village, because all the visitors looked at him and not at the cute little cottages. Some of the Japanese visitors even took pictures of him. Roy stood up to Miss Too-Tight-Snotty-Breeches and did the bravest thing I've ever seen anyone do. He whipped out his mobile phone and said, "Don't bother, I'll call the police myself!"

And he did. He actually phoned the police. I swear! I was so proud of him, but not proud enough to stick around. If the police were on their way, I was outta there!

I ran back home.

I always thought of home as a safe place. Like, when my friends tease me and I've had enough, I say, "Sorry, but I have to go home now." Or, when I'm watching TV and I hear about an earthquake somewhere, I think, "Wow, sure am glad I'm home and not there."

So, I was at home, where everything was supposed to feel safe, but everything felt lousy.

It started with my Dad. He was in a really bad mood because Amelia hadn't shown up for work at the Post Office. When I got home, he said, "Bruce, I need you to go to the hardware shop and buy some rat traps. We discovered a rat in here today."

"No, Dad! Don't kill the rat! I can explain everything."

Dad wouldn't listen to me, though. He just said, "Go and buy some traps before the hardware shop closes."

"But, Dad..."

"Go!"

So I went to the hardware shop and bought a rat trap, hoping and praying that it wouldn't crush poor Amelia. I had to do something to stop it from happening.

When I got back to the Post Office, I discovered a Police Officer was there. So was Roy, his parents, and Miss Too-Tight-Snotty-Breeches and her evil eye.

The Police Officer said, "I need to have a word with you," but, believe me, it was many words and they were mostly to my parents.

"Your friend here claims that the two of you were in the Model Village after hours the other evening and saw the missing alpaca there. Can you substantiate this?"

I didn't know what substantiate meant. It sounded important and I didn't wanna mess this up. So I turned to my Dad and said, "I don't know what that word means."

Even my Dad was giving me the evil eye. "Is what he's saying the truth?"

Okay, I know I'm supposed to tell the truth, the whole truth and nothing but the truth, but I also knew that, on this occasion, the truth would get me into serious trouble. Go Directly to Gaol. Do Not Pass Go. Do Not Collect £200. So I decided to go with the second best option, which was to stretch the truth. "Well, we go to the Model Village a lot," I said. "Let's see, when was the last time we were there? Hmmm...I'm trying to remember..."

Roy glared at me. "Tell them! We saw Thumpet. They shrunk him."

Miss Too-Tight-Snotty-Breeches was still giving me the evil eye.

While everyone waited for me to answer, the Police Officer blabbed the whole story to my parents: "Roy claims that they saw the alpaca and that it has shrunk to twelve centimetres. He also claims that there are small people living in the Model Village, who are only about so high..." He gestured fifteen centimetres.

"I've got pictures to prove it," said Roy, handing the officer some pictures.

The Police Officer just looked at them and smiled. "Good photos," he said. Then he looked at the parents and said, "My kids have a picture where my head is on the body of a sumo wrestler. It's amazing what they can do in Photoshop these days."

The way the Police Officer talked to our parents made me realize he thought our story was bogus.

My Dad asked me, "Well, son, what do you have to say about this?"

"Nothing."

Roy shouted at me, "Bruce! Tell them the truth. Tell them what you saw."

Everyone glared at me. I felt terrible. But I didn't say a word.

The Police Officer thanked my parents and said, "Sorry to

have bothered you. Hope you catch that rat. Pesky rodents!"

Then Roy's parents apologized and said that they would follow up to see if anybody else knew anything more about their missing alpaca, and I don't remember what else was said because the only thing I remember is how angry Roy was at me. I ran upstairs to my bedroom and locked the door.

A couple of hours later, I got an email from Roy. It said: "I hate you. You're one of them. A small person."

He was right. I was a small person.

It was the worst day of my life.

Chapter Fourteen
(Not Thirteen)

YOU may have noticed I left out Chapter Thirteen. That's because thirteen is an unlucky number. So let's just skip ahead to Chapter Fourteen. Okay?

I saw a cool show on television once about avalanches. You know, where tons of snow comes CRASHING DOWN! So, let's pretend you're taking a nice walk in the mountains...la-di-dah...and thinking, gee this snow sure is pretty, then all of a sudden – WHOOSH! You're under a huge pile of snow. Avalanche!

That's what it felt like being a small person. Roy was mad at me. In school he wouldn't even look at me, so I emailed him about a million times and used up all of my minutes on my mobile phone leaving messages. That made my Dad mad at me. "How many times do I have to tell you? Emergencies only!" My Mom was still mad at me about the whole Police Officer thing. Everyone in the universe was mad at me.

Avalanche!

It's all because I'm a small person. Let me explain – I'm not talking about height here. Roy and I are almost the same height, but he's a big person and I'm a small person. It's all about attitude.

Roy is honest and brave and will do whatever is right. That's big.

And a small person is a coward and a liar and someone not worthy of a big friend like Roy. That's me.

I had let him down. I felt lousy. How could I have done that to my best friend in the whole world? Roy deserves a better friend than, well, me.

Small.

I wanted to prove to Roy that I can be big, too. But how? I can tell you first-hand, it's hard for a small person to think big.

I went home to figure it out but I was totally surprised to see Roy's Mum sitting in the dining room with my Mom. They were having tea and yak, yak, yakking. When my Mom saw me, she sent me up to my bedroom, but I crept out so I could spy on them. This is what I overheard:

Roy's Mum: "I'm so worried about him. First, he made up stories about talking to the alpacas, and now one of them has gone missing. And stories about witches and little people living in the Model Village and, dear me, what do you make of it all?"

My Mom: "Oh, he's just a kid with a vivid imagination, that's all. Bruce has told a tall tale or two himself...blah, blah, blah..." (This is the part where my Mom felt the need to tell Roy's Mum everything that is wrong with me. But I'll spare you the gory details.)

Later, at dinner, my Dad was still upset about Amelia. "It's not like her not to show up for work. She hasn't called. Nothing."

I wanted to explain, but what's the point? They don't believe a word I say.

Finally, he changed the subject. He said to my Mom, "So what did Tess want?" (Translation: Tess is Roy's Mum.) Then he looked at me and said, "Or should we have this discussion later?" (Translation: so Big Ears Bruce can't overhear us.)

"No, it's fine," said my Mom. "Tess came over because she's worried about the Victorian Late-night Shopping Event. It appears to be falling apart. Many shops are closing because staff refuse to work. Tess said she has hardly any volunteers willing to help. No one seems to be cooperating this year. She's so frustrated. She's asked us to help change people's minds."

My Dad said, "I'm afraid there are small minds at work in the village this year. Small people set in their ways. Pity, because it could be such a wonderful evening."

I had to speak up. I couldn't hold it in any longer. "I know whose fault it is. It's Mrs. Nethercote's!"

My Dad said, "You mustn't blame her, son. She's not responsible for all the small-minded people in the village."

"Yes, she is," I said. "She shrunk them. She's a witch!"

My Dad just laughed. "Well, that's a polite word for her."

"No, it's true, I swear. Roy was telling the truth. I saw the little people, too. And it's all the fault of the Witch-on-the-Water!"

Even after my mini-meltdown I still don't think my parents believed a word I said. It's because I'm one of the small people. No one will ever believe me until I become big. But how do I do that?

That's the big question.

At school the next day it was National Mobile Phone Vibrating Day. Even though there's a strict rule at school – no mobile phones during school hours – text messages flew back and forth. The following day, Friday, was supposed to be the Victorian Late-night Shopping Event, but the text message going around was: VLNSE NOT!

Was it true? Or was this just another lame rumour like the one going around a few weeks ago about an asteroid that was supposed to collide with Earth? So I wasn't ready to jump aboard this rumour train yet.

Roy would know if it was true or not. But Roy was the one person I couldn't ask. Man, not being friends really bites!

After school, I went to the grocery shop where Roy goes to buy sweets. I didn't go there to see Roy, I went because, well, just because I felt like it. So I was just hanging out near the sweets when I overheard all these people talking about the Victorian Late-night Shopping Event. "Did you hear?" and "Yes, it's such a shame" or "I'm not surprised." Hey, maybe the rumour was true? Maybe it had been cancelled?

I figured my Dad would know for sure. He's the village Postmaster and he knows everything. So I went back home to the Post Office and that's when I nearly had a heart attack! I saw Dad talking to – you won't believe it - the Witch-on-the-Water!

I'm not lying!!!

Was she ratting me out? Was she making threats that, if I didn't stop spying on her, she was going to shrink me and stuff me in a cage, too?

I ran out of the Post Office and hid in the alley until the Witch-on-the-Water was gone. Okay, I know I'm a coward and a small person and I wanted to do the big thing, really I did, but it's hard when you're up against the Witch-on-the-Water.

The rumour was true. The Victorian Late-night Shopping Event was cancelled. At dinner, it was all my parents talked about. They were bummed out, too. Not only because they think it's lots of fun, like I do, but because it means no business. But Dad never mentioned a word about You-Know-Who coming to the Post Office.

Finally, I couldn't hold it back any longer. "Dad, what did Mrs. Nethercote want?" I braced myself for the bad news...

"She bought some stamps. Why do you ask?"

Stamps?????!!! "That's all?"

"Well, perhaps she came to the village to celebrate the cancellation of the late-night shopping. She finally got her way. I've never seen her so happy."

My Mom said, "Oh, that woman won't be happy until she cancels Christmas, too."

My Dad laughed.

I didn't.

Does the Witch-on-the-Water have that kind of power? Could Christmas now be on the Endangered Holiday List?

Avalanche!

Chapter Fifteen

BAH-humbug!

The next day at school, everyone was totally narked about the Victorian Late-night Shopping Event being cancelled. So, to cheer us up, Mrs. Jenkins read us "A Christmas Carol" by some old bloke named Charles Dickens. In the story there's this mean old guy named Scrooge who hates Christmas (wonder if he's related to Mrs. Nethercote?) and he always says, "Christmas! Bah-humbug!"

A Bah-humbug Christmas - that's what we were having this year in Bourton-on-the-Water. There was no village Christmas tree in the river, no lights, no decorations in the shop windows. I even missed the mistletoe – how sad is that?

After school I went home and, before I could even drop my coat on the floor, my Mom said, "Mrs. Dorsey needs your help. I told her you'd come over straightaway."

For your info, Mrs. Dorsey is Roy's grandmother. (He calls her Nan Olga.) She lives in Tam O'Shanter Cottage on Bow Lane, not too far from us. She always needs Roy to help her do stuff like set a mousetrap, or take out the rubbish, or both - sometimes we have to give a nice funeral to a dead mouse before burying it in the Dustbin of Eternity. We usually do it together, but if Roy isn't around then I get the honours. But today I just didn't feel like it.

"Nah, can't be bothered," I said, and dropped my coat.

"Go," said my Mom. "Don't be so small."

There's that word again!

"And what did I tell you about dropping your coat on the floor?"

Why is it okay to leave my shoes on the floor but not my coat? Too many stupid rules!

So I knocked on Nan Olga's door and she opened it. "Well, look who's here." Once I walked inside, I realized she didn't say it to be polite; she said it to tell someone sitting at the table. Someone enjoying a plate of biscuits and a glass of milk. Someone named Roy.

"What's he doing here?" said Roy and, believe me, he did not sound happy.

Nan Olga paid no attention to him and said to me, "Do you want some biscuits and milk, too, dear?"

"No thanks." What I wanted was to run back home.

"Nonsense. Sit in the chair next to Roy Boy."

I sat down but neither of us said a word. Still, Nan Olga acted as if nothing in the world was wrong. La-di-da. She gave me some biscuits and a glass of milk, so I sucked it down, just to be polite.

Then Nan Olga handed me some huge platters and said, "Here, last week your mother asked to borrow these for the late-night shopping evening."

In the past, my Mom always served lots of Christmas goodies to customers during the Victorian Late-night Shopping Event.

"Never mind, she doesn't need them now," I said.

Roy said, "Haven't you heard, Nana? The shopping event has been cancelled."

Nan Olga said, "Well, it may have been cancelled, but I'm

still going out this evening. Aren't you two?"

"What's the point?" I said. "Nothing will be open."

"So what?" she said. "If I want to have a pleasant evening in the village, nothing will stand in my way."

I've gotta hand it to Nan Olga; she always looks on the bright side. Even when the bright side is dark and gloomy.

Roy said, "It's not a good idea, Nana. There's gonna be lots of witches and wizards coming to the village tonight. It's the Night of the Jackdaws."

"Oh really? Now why would witches and wizards want to come to Bourton-on-the-Water?"

So Roy told her the whole story – about Mrs. Nethercote; about the little people in the Model Village; about Thumpet – and, believe it or not, Nan Olga just smiled.

"Why are you trying to discourage me? You should be discouraging them – all those jackdaws."

Roy scratched his head. "How?"

Nan Olga said, "Well, I'd go ahead with the Christmas festivities if I were you – with the late-night shopping event. If the witches and wizards don't like it, let them go elsewhere. Why should you give up your special evening?"

Roy looked at me and I looked at him. Even though Roy totally hated my guts, I think we were thinking the same thought: she's so right!

Roy said, "But what about the village Christmas tree? It hasn't been put up or decorated or anything."

I agreed. "There won't be anyone singing Christmas carols."

"Nobody will be wearing Victorian costumes. It'll be totally Bah-humbug!"

Nan Olga gave us some more biscuits. "Well, you two could sing. You could wear costumes. You could decorate the tree."

I have to admit, it wasn't a lame idea. "Do you wanna?" I asked Roy.

"Got nothing better to do," he said.

We jumped up, and I grabbed us each another biscuit for the road (in case of an Energy Emergency). Roy gave Nan Olga a hug and we were outta there.

"Don't forget the platters," she said to me.

Oops, I almost did.

Roy and I walked to the village green. Lying next to the river was this huge tree, still wrapped in twine to protect its branches and stuff. It was supposed to be the village Christmas tree, but nobody had put it up yet. "How are we supposed to decorate it?" I asked. I mean, it was seriously big!

"We need a Christmas Tree Plan," said Roy.

Duh! But where were we supposed to find such a plan?

Roy said, "Take those platters to your Mum and go get your wellies. Then meet me back here in twenty minutes."

"Where are you going?" I asked.

"Back up to the farm to get the alpacas. We need their help. It's all part of the plan." He ran off.

"Wait!" I shouted, running after him. When I caught up I handed him the Energy Emergency biscuits. "Here, you'll need these."

Roy only took one. He left the other for me. He ran off shouting, "We're Team Christmas!"

Man, it felt great to be friends again. This was gonna be so much fun. I ate my emergency biscuit and ran home fast. (I nearly dropped the platters!)

By the time I got back to the river, Roy was already there with the alpacas and, of course, Alfie the sheep. Roy wore his wellies, too, but he had a serious look on his face – that meant he was hard at work thinking about the Christmas Tree Plan.

"Okay, so how is Team Christmas supposed to put up this humongous tree?" I asked.

Roy explained the Christmas Tree Plan to me, but please don't ask me to repeat it because it was very complicated. Basically, he told me to unwrap the tree. Okay, so I took off the twine. That was the easy part. Next, he wanted four long pieces of twine of equal length. The Christmas Tree Plan involved tying one end of the twine to the tree and the other end to an alpaca (or sheep). Then we were each to go in different directions while Roy pushed the tree up. He was pretty certain this would work.

Sounded weird to me but since I had No Christmas Tree Plan, I had to go along with Roy's. We got all the animals ready and Roy said, "Okay, go!" Then he said the same thing in Pacachatter.

We all did what we were told; all except for Alfie, that is - he followed Fluff.

"No, Alfie, go the other way," said Roy, but it was too late. The twines got all twisted up. What a mess!

That's when Mr. McKenney – he's a big cook with a big belly who works in one of the small tearooms in the village – stepped outside and said, "What do you lads think you're doing?"

"Putting up this tree," said Roy.

"Who said you could do that?"

"We're Team Christmas," said Roy, "and the Captain told us to put it up."

"And who might the Captain be?"

Roy pointed at me. I'm not kidding. At me!

Mr. McKenney laughed so hard I thought he was going to bust his big belly. "Perhaps I'd better help Team Christmas. Let me fetch my wellies." He went back into the kitchen.

Roy and I waited for Mr. McKenney to come back. We waited and waited and waited. The longer we waited the worse I felt.

"Do you think he's calling the police?" I said. "Maybe there's a law against putting up a Christmas tree without a licence or something?"

"Be real! They can't arrest us for putting up a Christmas tree," said Roy. "Can they?"

We were about to make a run for it when Mr. McKenney came back, bringing Mr. Pratley and his son, Geoff, with him. (Mr. Pratley owns the tearoom and Geoff is about fourteen and already growing a moustache. Serious!)

Mr. McKenney said, "Brought us some extra help." Then he rubbed his hands together and said, "Alright, Team Christmas, let's put up this tree."

Leave it to Mr. Pratley to see a flaw in the Christmas Tree Plan – we didn't have a base for the tree. (Hey, Team Christmas never said it was A Perfect Christmas Tree Plan.) So, while Mr. Pratley and his son, Moustache Boy, built a base, Mr. McKenney told Roy and me to fetch the Christmas tree lights. "I know right where they are," said Roy.

Roy and I and the alpacas headed over to the Tourist Information Office, where his Mum was working. I stayed outside with the alpacas because of the animal-discrimination rules. So Roy went inside by himself and told his Mum that we needed the lights for the village Christmas tree. (The lights are kept in the attic there, but you've got to promise not to tell anyone because that might be top secret.) Roy's Mum didn't believe him when we told her Team Christmas was putting up the tree, so she came outside to take a look for herself.

"Now do you believe us?" said Roy.

Roy's Mum gave us each a big hug in broad daylight. How embarrassing! She even gave Emily a hug around her long neck. Emily batted her eyes but I don't think she was embarrassed.

"I'm delighted," said Roy's Mum. "Let's go find those lights!"

Since the alpacas were part of Team Christmas, too, their job was to carry the boxes over to the river. We loaded them up and off they went. By the time we all got there, Mr. McKenney and Mr. Pratley and Moustache Boy had just finished building the base for the tree.

And Team Christmas was growing. Mr. Moss, who owns an art gallery, came out and said, "Can I help?" And Mr. Michaels offered to help, too. (He's retired, but not too tired to help.) So it wasn't long before The Massive Team Christmas had the village Christmas tree standing tall in the river.

As we strung the lights, Team Christmas sang 'Jingle Bells' and we were laughing all the way. When people walked past and saw the village Christmas tree in the river they were really happy and gave us a big thumbs-up.

Even the shopkeepers came out for a look. They all said "ooh and ahh" and stuff like that and Mrs. Silvester, who owns a sweet shop, said, "How sweet!" Does she have a one-track mind or what?

A few minutes later, a van with a big horse box attached drove into the village. But it wasn't a horse in the box, it was a reindeer! Roy and I checked it out. So did the alpacas and, of course, Alfie.

The driver said, "Do you kids know where I'm supposed to set up for tonight?"

"Let me go ask my Mum, she'll know," said Roy, and he and I ran over to the Tourist Information Office to get her while the alpacas stayed behind to sniff the reindeer.

Roy's Mum came back with us and said to the driver, "Oh, I'm so sorry to tell you this, but the evening has been cancelled. Didn't you hear?"

"Nobody told me," he said and, believe me, he was annoyed.

Just then, Roy came up with the best idea in the whole universe. "Mum, let's un-cancel it!"

"The Victorian Late-night Shopping Event? We can't. It's too late," she said. "All the shops will be closed."

"Not if Team Christmas convinces them to stay open. Look, the Christmas tree is up; the reindeer is here. If we start a phone tree, the entire village will be here. We can do it. I know we can."

I agreed. Totally.

Roy's Mum asked the driver, "Are you game?"

"I'm here," he said, "and Rudolph and I don't have anywhere else to go this evening."

Roy's Mum had the biggest smile I've ever seen. "Your arrival with the reindeer may turn out to be a most wonderful mistake," she said. "Park right here and set up the tent for the reindeer on the village green." Then she turned to Roy and me. "Okay, Team Christmas, we have our work cut out. We've got to put together the Victorian Late-night Shopping Event – in the next hour!"

"Brilliant," I said.

"Team Christmas is definitely up for the challenge," said Roy.

Roy's Mum said, "Alright, then, let's begin. Tie up the alpacas where they'll be out of mischief and then meet me over at Celestial Daze."

The alpacas weren't thrilled about being tied up next to a bench on the green, but Roy promised them, in Pacachatter, of course, that we'd be back soon.

Roy and I went to Celestial Daze, a gift shop in the centre of the village. Mr. and Mrs. Leonard own the shop and Roy's Mum asked them to stay open. That's when I realized that Team Christmas might have a tough job ahead.

"No," said Mr. Leonard. "What's the point? The evening has been cancelled."

Roy's Mum gave about a million reasons to stay open, but Mr. Leonard wouldn't do it. He had been bitten by the Bah-humbug.

So Roy's Mum said, "Thanks anyway," and pushed Roy and me towards the door.

"Wait," said Mrs. Leonard. "I have nothing planned for this evening. I'll keep the shop open. Let's see what happens." She gave us a big wink.

"Bless! Thank you," said Roy's Mum.

After that, we went next door to the clothing shop and asked the lady in charge to please stay open for the evening. She complained about not having any help and blah, blah, blah, but in the end she said, "Well, I suppose I could give it a go for a while."

We left her shop and Roy's Mum continued talking to shop-keepers while Roy and I started the Phone Tree.

This is how it worked: Roy and I went back to the Tourist Information Office and called five friends and told them to come to the Victorian Late-night Shopping Event. Then those five called five friends and spread the word. And so on and so on. If everyone did as they were told, the Phone Tree would be huge and lots of people would show up for the Victorian Late-night Shopping Event.

Even after I had called five people, I called more. (Sometimes I dialled a wrong number, but I told them to come, too. What the heck!) I've never talked to so many people in my life. I kept phoning people until I heard...

Five bongs!

St. Lawrence's church announced to the world that it was five o'clock. Time to close up the village. But please-oh-please-oh-please not tonight!

Roy and I ran outside to check. And guess what – the shops stayed open. (Well, most of them anyway.) And there were people in the village - lots of them! That meant the Phone Tree had worked! Everyone was so thrilled to see the village Christmas tree and the reindeer.

They were even thrilled to see the alpacas and made a fuss over them. Roy untied the alpacas so that they could hang out with us. And, best of all, you'll never believe who showed up...

"Father Christmas!"

Roy and I ran over to his sleigh and I said, "Guess news of the cancellation didn't reach the North Pole."

Father Christmas smiled and said, "Oh, I heard about it. But, remember, I always check my lists twice." (That's why he's so brilliant!) And then he offered us a ride in his sleigh.

Roy and I took a very cool yuletide ride to the other end of the village with the alpacas and, of course, Alfie the sheep trotting right behind us.

From there, we went over to the Coronation Bridge, where the village Pantomime Group were singing Christmas carols. "Fa la la la la..." and all that stuff. Every singer wore a Victorian costume and held a candle. I thought they sounded pretty good, but I'm sure Simon Cowell would say, "Hideous, simply hideous."

Just then, Roy pointed to something across the village green. Something bundled in a coat, hat, scarf, muff, and mittens. "Look, there's Nan Olga," he said.

"Where?"

How he could tell that his grandmother was under that bundle, I'll never know. We went over to see her and Roy said, "Look at the tree, Nana. Isn't it beautiful? We helped put it up."

"Did you?" said Nan Olga. "Now where did you get a big idea like that?" She gave us each a wink and a smile.

The evening was so much fun; that is, until I saw something overhead that gave me the creeps. Jackdaws! Dozens of huge black birds circled the sky above the village green.

I shuddered.

And not because it was cold outside.

Chapter Sixteen

JACKDAWS circled above the village green for several minutes, then flew off towards the cemetery. Roy noticed them, too, and asked me, "Do you think all the people on the green scared them off?"

"Yeah," I said. "Tonight the green totally belongs to Team Christmas!" As much as I wanted to believe it, I have to confess, I really didn't.

But the jackdaws were gone and the Victorian Late-night Shopping Event was happening and it was a major blast. Even street vendors were there, selling cool stuff like necklaces that glow in the dark and battery-powered Christmas Stockings that blink and play Jingle Bells. Even red and green candyfloss. And, of course, that horrible smoochy-smoochy stuff – mistletoe. (Thumbs down!!!)

I'm proud to say the Phone Tree was a total success. There were loads of people in the village and they were all having fun. Shopping. Singing. Pigging out.

I checked in with my parents. They were working at the Post Office but even they were having fun. They wore Victorian costumes and didn't care that they looked really old-fashioned. Dad said he and Mom were supposed to be characters from that book Mrs. Jenkins had just read us. The Bah-humbug one. They pretended to be Bob Cratchit and his wife. "We even have a crutch for you, Tiny Tim!"

"No way!" I was outta there!

I joined Roy again out on the village green, where we hung out with the alpacas. All of a sudden, Alfie hid behind Emily, like he didn't want to be seen. That's because Roy's Dad and his sister, Chloe, joined us. They had walked to the village and Roy's father wore a rucksack with wires and stuff hanging out.

"What's in there?" asked Roy.

"The Super Sheep Sleep 'n' Fleecer," said Roy's Dad. "I'm hoping the scouts from 'The Dragons' Den' are here."

No wonder Alfie was hiding. He's a sheep who wants to be an alpaca, not a guinea pig.

Roy's Mum and Nan Olga joined us, too. Roy's Dad gave Roy's Mum a hug.

"Hey, what a night," he said. "You should be proud."

Roy's Mum turned to Roy and me and said, "I didn't pull this event off by myself. All the credit goes to Team Christmas."

That made Roy and me feel great. We smiled and Nan Olga asked Roy to take a picture and it was one of those mushy moments until Chloe said, "No way! I'm outta here before any of my friends sees me with you freaks."

Hey, she's thirteen and doesn't want to be seen with boys, alpacas, and a geeky father wearing a rucksack with wires hanging out. Who can blame her?

Even Roy's dad left – he wanted to see if the scouts had shown up yet.

So Roy said, "We're outta here, too, Mum."

"Have fun, Team Christmas," she said.

Roy and I and the alpacas and, of course, Alfie the sheep went off to have fun, but we remembered Thumpet wasn't with us. And that's when, all of a sudden, it was like a giant vacuum had sucked all the fun out of the air!

It began with the alpacas. They began to sniff, sniff, sniff. They were sniffing like crazy. And snorting and bouncing up and down.

"What's the matter?" asked Roy, in Pacachatter, of course. It's like the alpacas were on alert - their ears perked straight up!

And that's when Roy told me, "They smell trouble."

I pretended not to hear. "Wanna go get a hot chocolate?" I asked.

But Roy pretended not to hear me. "We better check it out."

If it was trouble we were looking for, it wasn't hard to find.

"Go home! All of you – be gone!" It was Mrs. Nethercote! The Witch-on-the-Water blew into the village like a storm, using her stick as a threat, not a crutch. She pushed her way through the crowd gathered on the green. "Go home! You have no business here! This night belongs to the Jackdaws!"

"Uh oh!" I can't remember if it was me who said it or Roy. Didn't matter. It was trouble with a stick.

The Witch-on-the-Water shouted and pushed her way past little kids busy looking at the reindeer. The kids were so scared they grabbed hold of their mothers' legs. But the Witch-on-the-Water didn't stop there; she stomped towards the Coronation Bridge. Roy and I and the alpacas followed, keeping a safe distance, to be sure.

The Pantomime Group stood on the bridge, holding candles, singing a Christmas carol, when the Witch-on-the-Water shouted: "Quiet! Stop that noise! Go home! All of you!"

A visitor who was listening to the singing turned to her. "Hush, madam! How rude!"

Man, talk about the wrong thing to say. The Witch-on-the-Water reminded me of a dragon that couldn't snort fire. She scratched her left knee and rubbed her right elbow.

"Uh oh!" I said.

"What's the matter?" asked Roy.

"Watch! Something horrible is about to happen."

And, sure enough, a sudden gust of wind blew out the flames

on the candles. But that wasn't the horrible part – this was: several singers fell off the bridge and – KER SPLASH – right into the river below. Some people screamed but others had the good sense to help the poor wet singers out of the water. Man, talk about dripping!

Roy pulled me aside. "How did you know that would happen?"

"Because of the Witch-on-the-Water," I said. "Didn't you see her scratch her knee? And rub her elbow? I saw her do it at the Chit Chat Café and to Alfie. That's how she jinxes people."

Roy was impressed. "Good work."

That felt good, too.

Anyway, the music had definitely stopped, and the singers became wringers – wringing out their cold wet clothes. Most headed for home. I didn't blame them. But, in all the excitement, we had lost track of the Witch-on-the-Water.

"Where'd she go?"

Roy spotted her – headed for the sleigh ride. "Let's follow."

There were tons of kids standing in a queue, waiting to have a ride with Father Christmas on his sleigh. He takes two at a time, dumps them off at the other end of the village, and then brings two more back. A horse pulls the sleigh, not a reindeer, because all the reindeer are resting up for the big night coming up at the end of the month.

"Ho, ho, ho, who's next?" said Father Christmas.

Jason pushed his way to the front of the queue and jumped on the sleigh ahead of a little girl who had been waiting for a long time. Such a gimp!

The Witch-on-the-Water shouted, "Stop that sleigh! Stop it at once!" She scared the little kids. Several dropped their candy-floss, especially after she yelled, "Get out of the village! All of you! Leave – before the jackdaws arrive."

Father Christmas said, "Madam, please, you're frightening the children."

"Good!" she said. "And get this dangerous sleigh out of here, too."

"Nonsense," said Father Christmas, jolly as can be. "There's no danger here. We're only going from hither to yon."

The Witch-on-the-Water said, "What if a car crashes in to you? Or a lorry? It could be a disaster."

"Oh, but the High Street is closed to traffic," said Father Christmas. "We'll be safe." And then he nudged the horse and off they went. Jason raised his arms in the air like it was a roller-coaster or something. Gimp, gimp, gimp.

Both Roy and I watched the Witch-on-the-Water as she fumed like a volcano ready to blow. She scratched her nose and tugged her ear...

Roy ran after Father Christmas and yelled, "Danger! Danger!"

Sure enough, the horse went down and the sleigh skidded and fell over. Father Christmas and a little kid and Jason fell out onto the High Street. I'm not kidding! People screamed. The little kid cried. It was Nightmare on High Street, starring Jason the gimp!

A shopper helped Father Christmas to his feet and several parents rushed to help the kid. No one was hurt - not even that gimp Jason - but everyone was upset. Roy helped the horse get back on its feet and I did what I do best - stayed out of the way.

One of the parents said, "Perhaps this sleigh ride wasn't such a good idea."

Someone else said, "Did anyone inspect this sleigh? How did this happen?"

One man turned to Roy. "How did you know this was going to happen?" he asked. "Why did you yell 'Danger'?"

Roy said, "Because it's all HER fault!" He pointed towards...towards....

She was gone! The Witch-on-the-Water was nowhere to be seen. But what we could see were birds. Jackdaws. Lots of them, flying in a circle above the green. They were back.

Roy said to me, "Hurry, we've got to find her!" We left the scene of the crime and searched the crowd for an out-of-control witch. The alpacas tagged along. As we looked for her we could overhear people talking. The jackdaws frightened people. Everyone was fed up, because the best night of the year was starting to go sour. Wet singers, crashing sleighs, scary birds flying above – what was next?

Near the Victoria Hall, we found Roy's Dad. He was talking to two guys, showing them the gizmo in his rucksack. Roy interrupted, saying, "Dad, you've got to help us..."

Roy's Dad said, "Son, can't you see I'm busy? These scouts are interested in my Super Sheep Sleep 'n' Fleecer."

Roy didn't care. "It's Mrs. Nethercote. She's the one causing the problems. You've got to stop her."

Roy's Dad looked real annoyed. (I know because my Dad gets the same look on his face.) He said, "What do you expect me to do? She's just a cranky old lady."

"But she's not. She's a witch! And do you see all these jack-daws? They're witches and wizards, too. They're about to do something horrible here."

Roy's Dad shook his head and said, "Son, they're just a flock of birds. That's all. Let's all try and get along this evening, alright?" He turned back to the two scouts and said, "Sorry, where was I?"

In other words, he blew us off! Totally!

The alpacas hummed and snorted and nudged Roy. They got his attention because they had found the Witch-on-the-Water in the crowd. "Oh, no!" said Roy, "Now look what she's doing!"

The Witch-on-the-Water was pulling down the village Christmas tree! Yes, the one we had worked so hard to put up! She was tugging on a rope that secured it.

"Stop it!" Roy shouted.

"Quiet, you," she growled back at him. "If this tree is down, perhaps everyone will go home – where they belong."

By the time I got there, the tree was swaying back and forth big time.

A visitor noticed the Witch-on-the-Water, too. "Hey, lady, what do you think you're doing?" He tried to stop her, but she struck him with her stick. He walked away, shaking his head. "Whacko!"

The Witch-on-the-Water went back to topple the tree, but Moustache Boy saw her.

"Hey, stop it, lady!" he shouted. "I worked hard to put that tree up." (Can you believe he took all the credit!? No mention of Team Christmas!)

Anyway, Moustache Boy went over to stop her and they had a tug-of-war with the ropes, but that only made the Witch-on-the-Water angrier. She let go of the ropes to scratch her elbow and tap her knee. Suddenly, Moustache Boy let go of the ropes and started to squirm. Something was weird. Something was inside Moustache Boy's coat. He unzipped it and all of these spiders crawled out. He totally freaked out. Spiders crawled out of his coat and covered his moustachy face. Totally gross! He screamed and ran, trying to escape the spiders.

The Witch-on-the-Water just laughed and went back to pulling on the rope and Roy...Wait, where was Roy?

I looked for him but he was gone. Vanished! Only Alfie the sheep was standing beside me. And we were alone with...the Witch-on-the-Water! Oh my gosh!

Finally, I saw Roy, but he was over on the other side of the river. He had sneaked over while Moustache Boy distracted the Witch-on-the-Water. He and the two alpacas, Fluff and Emily, pulled on the rope on the opposite side, trying to keep the village Christmas tree from swaying.

Once the Witch-on-the-Water noticed this, it didn't help

her seriously bad mood. "Let go, you brat!" she shouted. "This tree is coming down!"

Roy shouted something in Pacachatter.

All of a sudden, Alfie bleated and charged at the Witch-on-the-Water, butting his head into her. "Umph!" She fell to the ground.

Man, I laughed so hard! Even though Alfie wants to be an alpaca, he did what a sheep does best. He came back to me and I bent over to rub his head. "Way to go, Alfie!" I said. "That was even better than the first time you ran into her. Ha ha ha..."

"What's so funny?"

I looked up and there she was! The Witch-on-the-Water - in my face!! And she was angry. Nostrils-flaring angry! Fire-in-her-eyes angry!! Eu, her eye had that creepy flap over it. What do you call it? Pterygium-something-or-other.

I'm pretty sure I stopped laughing.

"Help me!" she snarled. "Get this tree down, then clear out the village. No one must be here. The Night of the Jackdaws is about to begin."

I think I shook my head. Actually, I think my entire body shook. All I remember is: I-HAVE-NEVER-BEEN-SO-SCARED-IN-MY-ENTIRE-LIFE!

The Witch-on-the-Water sniffed. Sniff, sniff, sniff. "Do I smell fear?" Then she crossed her arms and clicked her heels and – I'm not kidding – her head spun around in a complete circle!

And then she started to grow. Big and BIGGER. Everything was growing bigger. Everything all around me...

WAIT!!!....Hold on a second...

She wasn't growing bigger - I was SHRINKING! Oh my gosh...I was shrinking, shrinking, shrinking. Down, down, down. Everything became huge. The next thing I knew the Witch-on-the-Water looked like the King Kong of Witches.

She looked down at me and she was really giving me the evil

eye. "Now do as you are told!"

I nodded my head. I was too scared to disobey. She told me to hold the rope but I was too little to help. To me the rope was huge. So she clicked her elbows together and spun her head in the other direction. That's when the village Christmas tree came crashing down! It splashed in the river and the lights went out.

Everyone gasped. Then people screamed. Then they panicked. One old lady fainted. People scattered, especially when the jackdaws circling above started to swoop down on people. The birds nosedived the crowd. Seriously! In my small condition, I was afraid someone might step on me, so I hid underneath Alfie. From under there, it seemed like total chaos in the village but, to be honest, mostly what I saw were shoes! Shoes running in every direction. People were frightened, children were crying. Rats as big as me ran to and fro. Then I saw a shoe that looked familiar. I tugged on the trouser leg above it.

"Roy! Down here!" I tugged again.

"Bruce???" He dropped to his knees. "Is that you??? Oh no! What happened?"

"She smalled me."

Roy picked me up and held me in his hand. I've never seen him so upset. "This is horrible! The worst thing that could have happened." He was very careful to carry me over to the alleyway between two tearooms, away from the village Christmas tree disaster. "Don't worry," he said, sounding very worried. "I'll figure something out." The alpacas had followed us and they were upset, too. They snorted and squealed and bounced up and down. Roy understood them and said, "I agree. We've got to do something. She can't get away with this."

"Yeah, but what?"

"Think!" Roy closed his eyes and put his other hand to his forehead. "What do we know about witches? What did the website say?"

I wracked my tiny brain. "Let me think...let's see...witches prey on the wheat and the vegetables...."

"No, the weak and the vulnerable," said Roy.

"Yeah, right, whatever."

"But we're no competition for her," said Roy. "How can we make her weak and vulnerable?"

Fluff snorted. To little me, he seemed all worked up over something. The other alpacas snorted and hummed, too. Roy talked to them in Pacachatter.

"No, it would never work," he said.

"What?"

Roy explained. "The alpacas have an idea, but it's crazy. Dangerous."

"What is it?"

Fluff snorted some more. Alfie bleated something fierce.

Man, I wish I could understand Pacachatter. "Tell me! What are they saying?"

"They want us to scare the Witch-on-the-Water. Make her think we're more powerful than she is."

"For real? How can we do that? Especially now that I'm mini-me."

"Fluff has a plan and Alfie thinks it will work. Maybe we should give it a try?"

"What's the plan?"

"Don't ask!" said Roy. "Just hang out in my pocket and wish me luck. I'm gonna need it."

The next thing I knew I was being shoved inside Roy's coat pocket. (Phew – to be honest, it was kinda smelly!) But I could see all the action from there.

"Are you okay in there?" asked Roy.

"Yeah, sure, but..."

A crowd had gathered near the river, trying to figure out why the Christmas tree had fallen, and that's where Roy headed. He pushed his way through the crowd. "Dad! Dad!"

Roy found his Dad near the Perfumery and said, "Dad, we've got to stop Mrs. Nethercote. She's turning this into a Victorian Late-night Slasher Movie!"

Peeking out from inside Roy's coat pocket, I could see his Dad was flustered.

"What? What can I do?" said Roy's Dad.

Roy pulled the rucksack from his father's back. "I need to borrow this, Dad," he said. "It's important, I promise."

"Roy! Bring that back!"

But we were outta there.

We found the Witch-on-the-Water over on the far side of the green, away from the crowd, over at the War Memorial. Jackdaws circled above and several landed on the War Memorial. It wasn't long before the memorial was covered in jackdaws. There were more birds on the memorial than in all of Birdland. And that's a lot!

The alpacas pushed Roy forward and snorted at him. "Okay, okay, be patient," he said. I could see him building his courage.

"You can do it, Roy," I said. "I know you can!"

Roy took a couple of deep breaths. "Okay, pal, here goes nothing..."

He walked straight over to the War Memorial. The Witch-on-the-Water was climbing up the monument, using her stick for help. There were hundreds of black jackdaws covering the monument, and out of all that blackness there emerged all these wizards and warlocks, all wearing long robes and big pointed hats. Several of them helped the Witch-on-the-Water up to the top of the monument.

Roy shouted, "Stop, Mrs. Nethercote! I demand you make my friend big again!"

I don't think she could see me hiding in his coat pocket.

"Go away," she said. "I'm about to put this shopping event to an end once and for all." With the aid of one of the warlocks, she climbed to the highest level of the War Memorial.

"No, you've done quite enough damage for one night," said Roy. Man, I couldn't believe how brave he was.

The Witch-on-the-Water put down her stick and crossed her arms like she was about to cast her biggest spell ever. "And who's going to stop me?"

"Me," said Roy. "Here, catch!"

Roy tossed her the headgear from the backpack and I was surprised that the Witch-on-the-Water actually caught it. "What's this?" she hissed.

"Your worst nightmare," said Roy, with a confidence even I believed. "It's my Dad's latest invention – the Bourton Wicked-Witch-Whacker!"

The Witch-on-the-Water just laughed. "Go away before I shrink you, too."

Roy held his Dad's gizmo and said, "Don't believe me? If I flip this switch, all of your spells will go up in smoke."

The Witch-on-the-Water paused and then said, "A silly machine, that's all."

Just then, the alpacas and Alfie the sheep started sniffing like crazy. And snorting.

Roy said, "Oh yeah? I told you these alpacas are special. They can smell your fear."

All of a sudden, the Witch-on-the-Water looked scared. I'm not kidding. As I peered out from the inside of Roy's pocket, I could see how scared she looked. Maybe the alpacas could smell her fear?

Just then, Alfie rammed Roy, causing him to flip the switch.

In an instant the Witch-on-the-Water was aglow with blue currents of electricity running up and down her body. She reminded me of an electrical display I saw at a Science Fair once – only way more radical. She shrieked, "Ahhhhh!!!" Her hair stood straight on end. Amazing.

Roy cranked up the Super Sheep Sleep 'n' Fleecer as high as it would go. The Witch-on-the-Water shook, vibrated, and buzzed. And soon she started to shrink. And shrink. And then she sprouted feathers. Black feathers. She hissed and cursed and then squawked like a bird.

Roy turned off the power switch. The electricity stopped and there was nothing left but a jackdaw. The alpacas rushed at the jackdaws on the War Memorial and the birds flew off, frightened. It was a flurry of feathers. Finally, the jackdaw that had been the Witch-on-the-Water struggled and limped along, but it too flew off into the night.

Only a walking stick was left behind.

Chapter Seventeen

As much as I wanted to celebrate what had just happened to the Witch-on-the-Water, I couldn't. That's because I couldn't move in Roy's pocket. Suddenly it was seriously tight.

Rip!

Not only did I rip Roy's pocket, but I tumbled out of his coat, knocking Roy over in the process!

"Hey, what's going on?" he asked.

I didn't know and it was all happening so fast I didn't know what to think.

But everything was getting smaller! Everything was shrinking! Oh no...

....Wait! That's because I was getting BIGGER again. For real!

"Look at you!" shouted Roy. "You're big again."

I was. Amazing! "How did this happen?" (Not that I was complaining!)

The alpacas hummed and snorted and their ears perked up.

Roy said, "The alpacas are right – we broke the Witch-on-the-Water's spell."

"We did?"

"We must have. And if it worked for you, let's see if it worked for Thumpet and all the other little people at the Model Village!"

We got up and raced over to the Model Village, but it was closed. No one was in the ticket kiosk, not even Miss Too-Tight-Snotty-Breeches. But I did notice another jackdaw in a tree nearby. Watching us. Giving us the evil eye.

I asked Roy, "Hey, do you think that's Miss Too-Tight-Snotty-Breeches up in the tree?"

Roy didn't answer me because he was too busy figuring out how to get inside the Model Village. We couldn't go back to Mr. Notgrove's garden behind the Model Village because we didn't have any rope. With Miss Too-Tight-Snotty-Breeches out of the way, Roy said, "Let's climb over the turnstile."

So, with the help of the alpacas, we did just that. We climbed up on Fluff's back and that was enough of a boost for us to reach the top. Up and over we went.

We sneaked into the Model Village, but it was kinda spooky. Even though lights were on, something didn't feel right. Like nobody was at home. Still, we were there to look for Thumpet, and that's what we did. Roy called out his name, in Pacachatter, of course.

Suddenly we heard a whisper. "Who goes there?"

We turned around. "Coach Bernie!"

Coach Bernie was hiding behind one of the small shops on the High Street. But it was big Coach Bernie, not small Coach Bernie. He seemed real nervous. "What are you lads doing here?"

"Looking for my alpaca, Thumpet," said Roy. "Do you know where he is?"

"He's in a barn," said Coach Bernie. "I'll show you. Follow me."

Coach Bernie tiptoed over to a small barn where Thumpet was being kept. But when we got there Thumpet wasn't in the barn; he was on the barn. He had broken through it. That's because he was big again, too.

"Thumpet!" Roy gave the alpaca a big hug around its long neck. The alpacas started humming and snorting and doing all that Pacachatter stuff. Thumpet looked pretty chuffed to see Roy, too. And that's when I noticed...

"Amelia!"

She was behind Thumpet. She rubbed her face with her hands, kind of like a rat. "What happened to my whiskers?" she asked. "And my tail? Where did it go?"

"You're not a rat anymore," I told her. "The spell's been broken."

All of a sudden, other people rose from the background. They, too, were hiding behind small buildings and cottages in the Model Village. And they, too, were back to normal.

Mrs. Higgins was one of them. She had been hiding behind the small Baptist Church. She stepped out, delighted to be big again. She adjusted her blue wig and said, "Are you certain the spell's been broken?"

Roy explained what had happened at the War Memorial. The more he said, the more people gathered to listen. Big people. There were no more little people in the Model Village. And the more they heard, the more they liked what they heard.

"Is she gone for good?" asked Mrs. Hyde-Winthrop.

I shrugged. "We don't know for sure."

"Is it safe for us to leave?"

"I don't know," said Roy. "Let me check." He turned to Thumpet and asked a question in Pacachatter.

Thumpet sniffed. And then he sniffed some more. He went over to Mrs. Higgins and sniffed her.

"Oh! Careful, you brute!" she said.

Then he sniffed Mrs. Hyde-Winthrop. "Easy does it, big fella," she said.

Thumpet turned back to Roy and snorted. That's when Roy said, "Sorry, but you're still not safe."

"What?" I said. "Why not?" And I think I was speaking for the others as well.

Roy said, "Thumpet can still smell your fear. Alpacas can smell that, you know. For them, it's a good thing. But witches can smell fear, too. And it's fear that holds their spells together."

"So what can we do?" asked Amelia.

"Easy," said Roy. "Just let go of your fear."

Well, that was easy for Roy to say. That's because he's brave, but what about the rest of us?

Mrs. Higgins stepped forward. "Well, I, for one, am willing to give it a try. I'm tired of living in fear. I've lived my whole life that way. I've had quite enough, thank you. And here to prove it..." And with that, she removed her blue wig. She was as bald as an eagle.

Everyone gasped. Then they applauded. "Bravo! Good for you!"

Mrs. Higgins smiled. "That, my friends, was my worst fear. And look – I lived through it. Nothing can stop me now."

Coach Bernie stepped forward. "I'm letting go of my fear, too. I'm never gonna be small again."

Mrs. Hyde-Winthrop said, "I'm ashamed to admit that I was so afraid. Never again!"

One by one you could feel the little people were becoming big people again. It was amazing.

Roy turned to me and said, "What about you, Bruce? Can you do it?"

"I'm not sure," I admitted. "How do I do it?"

"Close your eyes and think of something big," said Roy.

Mrs. Higgins whispered in my ear, "And trust in your heart that you can do it."

So I closed my eyes and thought of the BIGGEST thing I could think of. And some way, somehow, I wasn't afraid anymore. I knew I could do it.

We all went to the turnstile to leave the Model Village, which definitely looked small to all of us big people. But the exit was locked.

"How do we get out of here?" asked Mrs. Hyde-Wright.

"I'll take care of it," said Roy. And I helped boost him up and over the turnstile.

A few minutes later, Roy returned with the owner of the Old New Inn.

"See, Mr. Collins," Roy said, "I told you Miss Too-Tight-Snotty-Breeches closed too early. Look at all the people she left inside. Even an alpaca!"

Mr. Collins was so flustered. He unlocked the exit turnstile and apologized to everyone. Even to Thumpet.

Everyone laughed. Big time.

Chapter Thirteen
(Not Eighteen)

NOW that I'm a BIG person again, I realize how silly it is to think 13 is an unlucky number. Come on, it's just a number! It's a good number. I can't wait until I'm thirteen – only two years to go!

Life is better BIG.

The Victorian Late-night Shopping Event was a big success, even though the Witch-on-the-Water had tried her best to ruin it. Everyone had a good time: some scoffed down fish 'n' chips, others maxed out their credit cards buying Christmas gifts, and couples even got to buy that mushy stuff called mistletoe. (Smooch-smooch!) But the big news is that the village Christmas tree was rescued. It took a big team to do it, but there were plenty of volunteers. The Christmas tree stood tall in the river and twinkled its lights for over a month.

My Dad said that this was one of the biggest holiday seasons ever. That means his business was good. And that makes him happy. When business is good I get an extra Christmas present or two. And that makes me happy.

Roy's Mum said that she's really busy over at the Tourist Information Office booking bed and breakfasts for next year's Victorian Late-night Shopping Event. She thinks it'll be bigger and better than ever.

Oh, before I forget, Roy's Dad went on that television programme, 'The Dragons' Den.' He had to repair the gizmo, because Roy had pretty much fried 'The Bourton Witch-Whacker.' But, once it was better than ever, Roy's Dad showed the Super Sheep Sleep 'n' Fleecer to the millionaire dragons. He took Alfie the sheep with him. Roy told me that poor Alfie was so scared to go on television that he didn't sleep for days before. So, by the time Roy's Dad used the gizmo on him in front of all the television cameras, Alfie was so tired he slept like a lamb. (That's a sheep joke, get it?) But when Alfie didn't wake up, that's when the millionaires decided not to invest in the Super Sheep Sleep 'n' Fleecer. "Pass!" Even though Roy's Dad was real disappointed, you'll be glad to know that Alfie woke up the next day and felt fine. He just needed a major nap, that's all. Still, it's back to the drawing board in the Shed of Invention for Roy's Dad. Roy and I felt bad for him because we know the gizmo works perfectly as a Bourton Wicked-Witch-Whacker. But, these days, how many witches need to be whacked? How many Bourton Wicked-Witch-Whackers would people buy? It's not like buying something everybody needs – like a skate-board or a Nintendo.

So far, no one has seen hide nor hair of the Witch-on-the-Water. Is she gone for good? I hope so. There were lots of rumours. People ask – Whatever happened to Mrs. Nether-cote? Where did she go? A nice family moved into her cottage and it's not so creepy anymore.

Miss Too-Tight-Snotty-Breeches was never seen again either. There's a new ticket-seller at the Model Village and she's very nice, but she complains a lot about a noisy jackdaw in a tree nearby. Wonder if it ever gives her the evil eye?

Are the Wizards and Warlocks coming back to Bourton? I don't know. I hope not. If they do, let's hope it's 200 years from now. I won't have to worry about it then.

Speaking of the Model Village, there were a few rumours about little people living there, but no one paid much attention. I asked my Dad why. He said, "Oh, it's just small talk, son. Big people don't pay attention to small talk."

But Roy and I knew the truth, and we saw big changes in some of the people who used to be small. Coach Bernie, for example. He resigned from our school so he could accept the position of Head Coach at a big university. He has big plans for the future. Good for him.

Mrs. Higgins was brave enough to quit her job at the grocery store and open her own shop. Okay, it's a small shop, but it's called, 'Mrs. Higgins' Big Wigs.' She sells wigs of every colour. Ladies seem to like her wigs a lot. So do circus clowns.

So, thanks to the Bourton Witch-Whacker, Bourton-on-the-Water is a nice place to visit again. Loads of visitors come to the village every day. They enjoy Birdland, the Dragonfly Maze, the Perfumery, the Motor Museum, the Model Railway and the Pottery, and, once they've seen absolutely everything in the village, they can pay money to see it all over again – only smaller – at the Model Village. But nobody should bother to peek in the windows because there are no more little people living in the Model Village anymore.

You'll be glad to know that the alpacas are still amazing. Fluff is as curious as ever and I'm sure he'll sniff out another mystery sometime soon. Emily hums a lot and always surprises me by how smart she is. She knows the postman is coming just by sniffing. Unreal! You'll be glad to know that Thumpet is no longer scared. He's still not very smart, though. The other day, Roy's Mum was hanging clothes out to dry and this time Thumpet got his neck tangled up in the clothes-line. Maybe Roy's Dad should invent a bigger brain for Thumpet?

Alfie-the-sheep's fleece is growing back. Looking pretty good. He still likes to hang out with the alpacas and the other sheep are cool about it. He's still an honorary alpaca.

Roy won a contest at school for "Best Photographer." It's a great picture he took at the Model Village, with big Mrs. Nethercote scaring little Mrs. Higgins as she flips her purple wig.

As for me, I'm living my life as big as possible. I'm lucky to have an amazing friend like Roy. Okay, I'm not nearly as smart as he is, and I don't speak Pacachatter, but I wasn't struck by lightning either. (And I'm kinda glad about that.)

I never told my parents that I was smalled. What's the point? I'm big now and getting bigger all the time. Remember when Roy told me to think of something big? Something I wanted but was afraid of? Wanna know what that thought was?

This story! I thought, I wanted to tell everyone about this amazing story, but I didn't think I was a smart enough fugle to write it. I was afraid I'd mess it up. But look – I did it! (Sorry if there are any misspelled words or bad sentences, but I'm still learning.)

Okay, now here's what I want you to do. Remember the Phone Tree? I want you to read this story and tell five friends to read it. Then make them promise to tell five friends and so on and so on. Soon everyone on the planet will read it. How cool is that?

If everyone thinks big thoughts, then think how great life will be. Fugles won't be afraid any more. Witches won't be able to prey on the weak and vulnerable. They'll have to settle for wheat and vegetables like everyone else.

Okay, I've gotta go now because Foggy has been waiting for me to finish this story so that I can take him out for a walk. He's at the door, whimpering, so that means he's really gotta go! Big time.

The NSPCC CHILDLINE

Telephone 0800 11 11

www. childline.org.uk